William Butler Yeats

Discoveries

Outlook

William Butler Yeats

Discoveries

1. Auflage | ISBN: 978-3-73261-844-6

Erscheinungsort: Paderborn, Deutschland

Erscheinungsjahr: 2018

Outlook Verlag GmbH, Paderborn.

THE COLLECTED WORKS OF WILLIAM BUTLER YEATS

DISCOVERIES. EDMUND SPENSER.
POETRY AND TRADITION; & OTHER
ESSAYS ☙ BEING THE EIGHTH VOLUME
OF THE COLLECTED WORKS IN VERSE
& PROSE OF WILLIAM BUTLER YEATS
☙ IMPRINTED AT THE SHAKESPEARE
HEAD PRESS STRATFORD-ON-AVON
MCMVIII

DISCOVERIES

PROPHET, PRIEST AND KING

THE little theatrical company I write my plays for had come to a west of Ireland town, and was to give a performance in an old ball-room, for there was no other room big enough. I went there from a neighbouring country- house, and, arriving a little before the players, tried to open a window. My hands were black with dirt in a moment, and presently a pane of glass and a part of the window-frame came out in my hands. Everything in this room was half in ruins, the rotten boards cracked under my feet, and our new proscenium and the new boards of the platform looked out of place, and yet the room was not really old, in spite of the musicians' gallery over the stage. It had been built by some romantic or philanthropic landlord some three or four generations ago, and was a memory of we knew not what unfinished scheme.

From there I went to look for the players, and called for information on a young priest, who had invited them and taken upon himself the finding of an audience. He lived in a high house with other priests, and as I went in I noticed with a whimsical pleasure a broken pane of glass in the fanlight over the door, for he had once told me the story of an old woman who a good many years ago quarrelled with the bishop, got drunk and hurled a stone through the painted glass. He was a clever man who read Meredith and Ibsen, but some of his books had been packed in the fire-grate by his housekeeper, instead of the customary view of an Italian lake or the coloured tissue-paper. The players, who had been giving a performance in a neighbouring town, had not yet come, or were unpacking their costumes and properties at the hotel he had recommended them. We should have time, he said, to go through the half- ruined town and to visit the convent schools and the cathedral, where, owing to his influence, two of our young Irish sculptors had been set to carve an altar and the heads of pillars. I had only heard of this work, and I found its strangeness and simplicity—one of them had been Rodin's pupil—could not make me forget the meretriciousness of the architecture and the commercial commonplace of the inlaid pavements. The new movement had seized on the cathedral midway in its growth, and the worst of the old and the best of the new were side by side without any sign of transition. The convent school was, as other like places have been to me—a long room in a workhouse hospital at Portumna, in particular—a delight to the imagination and the eyes. A new floor had been put into some ecclesiastical building and the light from a great mullioned window, cut off at the middle, fell aslant upon rows of clean and seemingly happy children. The nuns, who show in their own convents, where they can put what they like, a love of what is mean and pretty, make beautiful rooms where the regulations compel them to do all with a few colours and a few flowers. I think it was that day, but am not sure, that I had lunch at a convent and told fairy stories to a couple of nuns, and I hope it was not mere politeness that made them seem to have a child's interest in suchthings.

A good many of our audience, when the curtain went up in the old ball-room, were drunk, but all were attentive, for they had a great deal of respect for my friend, and there were other priests there. Presently the man at the door opposite to the stage strayed off somewhere and I took his place, and when boys came up offering two or three pence and asking to be let into the sixpenny seats, I let them join the melancholy crowd. The play professed to tell of the heroic life of ancient Ireland, but was really full of sedentary refinement and the spirituality of cities. Every emotion was made as dainty- footed and dainty-fingered as might be, and a love and pathos where passion had faded into sentiment, emotions of pensive and harmless people, drove shadowy young men through the shadows of death and battle. I watched it with growing rage. It was not my own work, but I have sometimes watched my own work with a rage made all the more salt in the mouth from being half despair. Why should we make so much noise about ourselves and yet have nothing to say that was not better said in that workhouse dormitory, where a few flowers and a few coloured counterpanes and the coloured walls had made a severe and gracious beauty? Presently the play was changed and our comedian began to act a little farce, and when I saw him struggle to wake into laughter an audience, out of whom the life had run as if it were water, I rejoiced, as I had over that broken window-pane. Here was something secular, abounding, even a little vulgar, for he was gagging horribly, condescendingto his audience, though not without contempt.

We had supper in the priest's house, and a government official, who had come down from Dublin, partly out of interest in this attempt 'to educate the people,' and partly because it was his holiday and it was necessary to go somewhere, entertained us with little jokes. Somebody, not, I think, a priest, talked of the spiritual destiny of our race and praised the night's work, for the play was refined and the people really very attentive, and he could not understand my discontent; but presently he was silenced by the patter of jokes.

I had my breakfast by myself the next morning, for the players had got up in the middle of the night and driven some ten miles to catch an early train to Dublin, and were already on their way to their shops and offices. I had brought the visitors' book of the hotel, to turn over its pages while waiting for my bacon and eggs, and found several pages full of obscenities, scrawled there some two or three weeks before, by Dublin visitors, it seemed, for a notorious Dublin street was mentioned. Nobody had thought it worth his while to tear out the page or block out the lines, and as I put the book away impressions that had been drifting through my mind for months rushed up into a single thought. 'If we poets are to move the people, we must reintegrate the human spirit in our imagination. The English have driven away the kings, and turned the prophets into demagogues, and you cannot have health among a people if you have not prophet, priest and king.'

———————————————

PERSONALITY AND THE INTELLECTUAL ESSENCES

M$_Y$ work in Ireland has continually set this thought before me: 'How can I make my work mean something to vigorous and simple men whose attention is not given to art but to a shop, or teaching in a National School, or dispensing medicine?' I had not wanted to 'elevate them' or 'educate them,' as these words are understood, but to make them understand my vision, and I had not wanted a large audience, certainly not what is called a national audience, but enough people for what is accidental and temporary to lose itself in the lump. In England, where there have been so many changing activities and so much systematic education, one only escapes from crudities and temporary interests among students, but here there is the right audience could one but get its ears. I have always come to this certainty: what moves natural men in the arts is what moves them in life, and that is, intensity of personal life, intonations that show them in a book or a play, the strength, the essential moment of a man who would be exciting in the market or at the dispensary door. They must go out of the theatre with the strength they live by strengthened with looking upon some passion that could, whatever its chosen way of life, strike down an enemy, fill a long stocking with money or move a girl's heart. They have not much to do with the speculations of science, though they have a little, or with the speculations of metaphysics, though they have a little. Their legs will tire on the road if there is nothing in their hearts but vague sentiment, and though it is charming to have an affectionate feeling about flowers, that will not pull the cart out of the ditch. An exciting person, whether the hero of a play or the maker of poems, will display the greatest volume of personal energy, and this energy must seem to come out of the body as out of the mind. We must say to ourselves continually when we imagine a character: 'Have I given him the roots, as it were, of all faculties necessary for life?' And only when one is certain of that may one give him the one faculty that fills the imagination with joy. I even doubt if any play had ever a great popularity that did not use, or seem to use, the bodily energies of its principal actor to the full. Villon the robber could have delighted these Irishmen with plays and songs, if he and they had been born to the same traditions of word and symbol, but Shelley could not; and as men came to live in towns and to read printed books and to have many specialised activities, it has become more possible to produce Shelleys and less and less possible to produce Villons. The last Villon dwindled into Robert Burns because the highest faculties had faded, taking the sense of beauty with them, into some sort of vague heaven and left the lower to lumber where they best could. In literature, partly from the lack of that spoken word which knits us to normal man, we have lost in personality, in our delight in the whole man—blood, imagination, intellect, running together—but have found a new delight, in essences, in states of mind, in pure imagination, in all that comes to us most easily in elaborate music. There are two ways before literature—upward into ever-growing subtlety, with Verhaeren, with Mallarmé, with Maeterlinck, until at last, it may be, a new agreement among refined and studious men gives birth to a new passion, and what seems literature becomes religion; or downward, taking the soul with us until all is simplified and solidified again. That is the choice of choices—the way of the bird until common eyes have lost us, or to the market carts; but we must see to it that the soul goes with us, for the bird's song is beautiful, and the traditions of modern imagination, growing always more musical, more lyrical, more melancholy, casting up now a Shelley, now a Swinburne, now a Wagner, are, it may be, the frenzy of those that are about to see what the magic hymn printed by the Abbé de Villars has called the Crown of Living and Melodious Diamonds. If the carts have hit our fancy we must have the soul tight within our bodies, for it has grown so fond of a beauty accumulated by subtle generations that it will for a long time be impatient with our thirst for mere force, mere personality, for the tumult of the blood. If it begin to slip away we must go after it, for Shelley's Chapel of the Morning Star is better than Burns's beer-house—surely it was beer, not barleycorn—except at the day's weary end; and it is always better than that uncomfortable place where there is no beer, the machine shop of the realists.

THE MUSICIAN AND THE ORATOR

Walter Pater says music is the type of all the Arts, but somebody else, I forget now who, that oratory is their type. You will side with the one or the other according to the nature of your energy, and I in my present mood am all for the man who, with an average audience before him, uses all means of persuasion—stories, laughter, tears, and but so much music as he can discover on the wings of words. I would even avoid the conversation of the lovers of music, who would draw us into the impersonal land of sound and colour, and would have no one write with a sonata in his memory. We may even speak a little evil of musicians, having admitted that they will see before we do that melodious crown. We may remind them that the housemaid does not respect the piano-tuner as she does the plumber, and of the enmity that they have aroused among all poets. Music is the most impersonal of things and words the most personal, and that is why musicians do not like words. They masticate them for a long time, being afraid they would not be able to digest them, and when the words are so broken and softened and mixed with spittle that they are not words any longer, they swallow them.

A GUITAR PLAYER

A GIRL has been playing on the guitar. She is pretty, and if I didn't listen to her I could have watched her, and if I didn't watch her I could have listened. Her voice, the movements of her body, the expression of her face, all said the same thing. A player of a different temper and body would have made all different, and might have been delightful in some other way. A movement not of music only but of life came to its perfection. I was delighted and I did not know why until I thought, 'That is the way my people, the people I see in the mind's eye, play music, and I like it because it is all personal, as personal as Villon's poetry.' The little instrument is quite light, and the player can move freely and express a joy that is not of the fingers and the mind only but of the whole being; and all the while her movements call up into the mind, so erect and natural she is, whatever is most beautiful in her daily life. Nearly all the old instruments were like that, even the organ was once a little instrument, and when it grew big our wise forefathers gave it to God in the cathedrals, where it befits him to be everything. But if you sit at the piano, it is the piano, the mechanism, that is the important thing, and nothing of you means anything but your fingers and your intellect.

THE LOOKING-GLASS

I HAVE just been talking to a girl with a shrill monotonous voice and an abrupt way of moving. She is fresh from school, where they have taught her history and geography 'whereby a soul can be discerned,' but what is the value of an education, or even in the long run of a science, that does not begin with the personality, the habitual self, and illustrate all by that? Somebody should have taught her to speak for the most part on whatever note of her voice is most musical, and soften those harsh notes by speaking, not singing, to some stringed instrument, taking note after note and, as it were, caressing her words a little as if she loved the sound of them, and have taught her after this some beautiful pantomimic dance, till it had grown a habit to live for eye and ear. A wise theatre might make a training in strong and beautiful life the fashion, teaching before all else the heroic discipline of the looking-glass, for is not beauty, even as lasting love, one of the most difficult of the arts?

THE TREE OF LIFE

WE artists have taken over-much to heart that old commandment about seeking after the Kingdom of Heaven. Verlaine told me that he had tried to translate 'In Memoriam,' but could not because Tennyson was 'too noble, too Anglais, and, when he should have been broken-hearted, had many reminiscences.' About that time I found in some English review an essay of his on Shakespeare. 'I had once a fine Shakespeare,' he wrote, or some such words, 'but I have it no longer. I write from memory.' One wondered in what vicissitude he had sold it, and for what money; and an image of the man rose in the imagination. To be his ordinary self as much as possible, not a scholar or even a reader, that was certainly his pose; and in the lecture he gave at Oxford he insisted 'that the poet should hide nothing of himself,' though he must speak it all with 'a care of that dignity which should manifest itself, if not in the perfection of form, at all events with an invisible, insensible, but effectual endeavour after this lofty and severe quality, I was about to say this virtue.' It was this feeling for his own personality, his delight in singing his own life, even more than that life itself, which made the generation I belong to compare him to Villon. It was not till after his death that I understood the meaning his words should have had for me, for while he lived I was interested in nothing but states of mind, lyrical moments, intellectual essences. I would not then have been as delighted as I am now by that guitar player, or as shocked as I am now by that girl whose movements have grown abrupt, and whose voice has grown harsh by the neglect of all but external activities. I had not learned what sweetness, what rhythmic movement, there is in those who have become the joy that is themselves. Without knowing it, I had come to care for nothing but impersonal beauty. I had set out on life with the thought of putting my very self into poetry, and had understood this as a representation of my own visions and an attempt to cut away the non- essential, but as I imagined the visions outside myself my imagination became full of decorative landscape and of still life. I thought of myself as something unmoving and silent living in the middle of my own mind and body, a grain of sand in Bloomsbury or in Connacht that Satan's watch fiends cannot find. Then one day I understood quite suddenly, as the way is, that I was seeking something unchanging and unmixed and always outside myself, a Stone or an Elixir that was always out of reach, and that I myself was the fleeting thing that held out its hand. The more I tried to make my art deliberately beautiful, the more did I follow the opposite of myself, for deliberate beauty is like a woman always desiring man's desire. Presently I found that I entered into myself and pictured myself and not some essence when I was not seeking beauty at all, but merely to lighten the mind of some

11

burden of love or bitterness thrown upon it by the events of life. We are only permitted to desire life, and all the rest should be our complaints or our praise of that exacting mistress who can awake our lips into song with her kisses. But we must not give her all, we must deceive her a little at times, for, as Le Sage says in *The Devil on Two Sticks*, the false lovers who do not become melancholy or jealous with honest passion have the happiest mistress and are rewarded the soonest and by the most beautiful. Our deceit will give us style, mastery, that dignity, that lofty and severe quality Verlaine spoke of. To put it otherwise, we should ascend out of common interests, the thoughts of the newspapers, of the market-place, of men of science, but only so far as we can carry the normal, passionate, reasoning self, the personality as a whole. We must find some place upon the Tree of Life high enough for the forked branches to keep it safe, and low enough to be out of the little wind-tossed boughs and twigs, for the Phœnix nest, for the passion that is exaltation and not negation of the will, for the wings that are always upon fire.

THE PRAISE OF OLD WIVES' TALES

A<small>N</small> art may become impersonal because it has too much circumstance or too little, because the world is too little or too much with it, because it is too near the ground or too far up among the branches. I met an old man out fishing a year ago, who said to me, 'Don Quixote and Odysseus are always near to me'; that is true for me also, for even Hamlet and Lear and Œdipus are more cloudy. No playwright ever has made or ever will make a character that will follow us out of the theatre as Don Quixote follows us out of the book, for no playwright can be wholly episodical, and when one constructs, bringing one's characters into complicated relations with one another, something impersonal comes into the story. Society, fate, 'tendency,' something not quite human, begins to arrange the characters and to excite into action only so much of their humanity as they find it necessary to show to one another. The common heart will always love better the tales that have something of an old wives' tale and that look upon their hero from every side as if he alone were wonderful, as a child does with a new penny. In plays of a comedy too extravagant to photograph life, or written in verse, the construction is of a necessity woven out of naked motives and passions, but when an atmosphere of modern reality has to be built up as well, and the tendency, or fate, or society has to be shown as it is about ourselves, the characters grow fainter, and we have to read the book many times or see the play many times before we can remember them. Even then they are only possible in a certain drawing-room and among such and such people, and we must carry all that lumber in our heads. I thought Tolstoi's 'War and Peace' the greatest story I had ever read, and yet it has gone from me; even Lancelot, ever a shadow, is more visible in my memory than all its substance.

THE PLAY OF MODERN MANNERS

OF all artistic forms that have had a large share of the world's attention, the worst is the play about modern educated people. Except where it is superficial or deliberately argumentative it fills one's soul with a sense of commonness as with dust. It has one mortal ailment. It cannot become impassioned, that is to say vital, without making somebody gushing and sentimental. Educated and well-bred people do not wear their hearts upon their sleeves and they have no artistic and charming language except light persiflage and no powerful language at all, and when they are deeply moved they look silently into the fireplace. Again and again I have watched some play of this sort with growing curiosity through the opening scene. The minor people argue, chaff one another, hint sometimes at some deeper stream of life just as we do in our houses, and I am content. But all the time I have been wondering why the chief character, the man who is to bear the burden of fate, is gushing, sentimental and quite without ideas. Then the great scene comes and I understand that he cannot be well-bred or self-possessed or intellectual, for if he were he would draw a chair to the fire and there would be no duologue at the end of the third act. Ibsen understood the difficulty and made all his characters a little provincial that they might not put each other out of countenance, and made a leading article sort of poetry, phrases about vine leaves and harps in the air it was possible to believe them using in their moments of excitement, and if the play needed more than that, they could always do something stupid. They could go out and hoist a flag as they do at the end of *Little Eyolf*. One only understands that this manner, deliberately adopted one doubts not, had gone into his soul and filled it with dust, when one has noticed that he could no longer create a man of genius. The happiest writers are those that, knowing this form of play is slight and passing, keep to the surface, never showing anything but the arguments and the persiflage of daily observation, or now and then, instead of the expression of passion, a stage picture, a man holding a woman's hand or sitting with his head in his hands in dim light by the red glow of a fire. It was certainly an understanding of the slightness of the form, of its incapacity for the expression of the deeper sorts of passion, that made the French invent the play with a thesis, for where there is a thesis people can grow hot in argument, almost the only kind of passion that displays itself in our daily life. The novel of contemporary educated life is upon the other hand a permanent form because having the power of psychological description it can follow the thought of a man who is looking into the grate.

HAS THE DRAMA OF CONTEMPORARY LIFE A ROOT OF ITS OWN?

I_N watching a play about modern educated people, with its meagre language and its action crushed into the narrow limits of possibility, I have found myself constantly saying: 'Maybe it has its power to move, slight as that is, from being able to suggest fundamental contrasts and passions which romantic and poetical literature have shown to be beautiful.' A man facing his enemies alone in a quarrel over the purity of the water in a Norwegian Spa and using no language but that of the newspapers can call up into our minds, let us say, the passion of Coriolanus. The lovers and fighters of old imaginative literature are more vivid experiences in the soul than anything but one's own ruling passion that is itself riddled by their thought as by lightning, and even two dumb figures on the roads can call up all that glory. Put the man who has no knowledge of literature before a play of this kind and he will say, as he has said in some form or other in every age at the first shock of naturalism, 'What has brought me out to hear nothing but the words we use at home when we are talking of the rates?' And he will prefer to it any play where there is visible beauty or mirth, where life is exciting, at high tide as it were. It is not his fault that he will prefer in all likelihood a worse play although its kind may be greater, for we have been following the lure of science for generations and forgotten him and his. I come always back to this thought. There is something of an old wives' tale in fine literature. The makers of it are like an old peasant telling stories of the great famine or the hangings of '98 or his own memories. He has felt something in the depth of his mind and he wants to make it as visible and powerful to our senses as possible. He will use the most extravagant words or illustrations if they suit his purpose. Or he will invent a wild parable, and the more his mind is on fire or the more creative it is, the less will he look at the outer world or value it for its own sake. It gives him metaphors and examples and that is all. He is even a little scornful of it, for it seems to him while the fit is on that the fire has gone out of it and left it but white ashes. I cannot explain it, but I am certain that every high thing was invented in this way, between sleeping and waking, as it were, and that peering and peeping persons are but hawkers of stolen goods. How else could their noses have grown so ravenous or their eyes so sharp?

WHY THE BLIND MAN IN ANCIENT TIMES WAS MADE A POET

A DESCRIPTION in the Iliad or the Odyssey, unlike one in the Æneid or in most modern writers, is the swift and natural observation of a man as he is shaped by life. It is a refinement of the primary hungers and has the least possible of what is merely scholarly or exceptional. It is, above all, never too observant, too professional, and when the book is closed we have had our energies enriched, for we have been in the mid-current. We have never seen anything Odysseus could not have seen while his thought was of the Cyclops, or Achilles when Briseis moved him to desire. In the heart of the greatest periods there is something careless and sudden in all habitual moods though not in their expression, because these moods are a conflagration of all the energies of active life. In primitive times the blind man became a poet as he becomes a fiddler in our villages, because he had to be driven out of activities all his nature cried for before he could be contented with the praise of life. And often it is Villon or Verlaine with impediments plain to all, who sings of life with the ancient simplicity. Poets of coming days, when once more it will be possible to write as in the great epochs, will recognise that their sacrifice shall be to refuse what blindness and evil name, or imprisonment at the outsetting, denied to men who missed thereby the sting of a deliberate refusal. The poets of the ages of silver need no refusal of life, the dome of many- coloured glass is already shattered while they live. They look at life deliberately and as if from beyond life, and the greatest of them need suffer nothing but the sadness that the saints have known. This is their aim, and their temptation is not a passionate activity, but the approval of their fellows, which comes to them in full abundance only when they delight in the general thoughts that hold together a cultivated middle-class, where irresponsibilities of position and poverty are lacking; the things that are more excellent among educated men who have political pre-occupations, Augustus Cæsar's affability, all that impersonal fecundity which muddies the intellectual passions. Ben Jonson says in the 'Poetaster,' that even the best of men without Promethean fire is but a hollow statue, and a studious man will commonly forget after some forty winters that of a certainty Promethean fire will burn somebody's fingers. It may happen that poets will be made more often by their sins than by their virtues, for general praise is unlucky, as the villages know, and not merely as I imagine—for I am superstitious about these things

—because the praise of all but an equal enslaves and adds a pound to the ball at the ankle with every compliment.

All energy that comes from the whole man is as irregular as the lightning, for the communicable and forecastable and discoverable is a part only, a hungry chicken under the breast of the pelican, and the test of poetry is not in reason but in a delight not different from the delight that comes to a man at the first coming of love into the heart. I knew an old man who had spent his whole life cutting hazel and privet from the paths, and in some seventy years he had observed little but had many imaginations. He had never seen like a naturalist, never seen things as they are, for his habitual mood had been that of a man stirred in his affairs; and Shakespeare, Tintoretto, though the times were running out when Tintoretto painted, nearly all the great men of the Renaissance, looked at the world with eyes like his. Their minds were never quiescent, never as it were in a mood for scientific observations, always an exaltation, never—to use known words—founded upon an elimination of the personal factor; and their attention and the attention of those they worked for dwelt constantly with what is present to the mind in exaltation. I am too modern fully to enjoy Tintoretto's Creation of the Milky Way, I cannot fix my thoughts upon that glowing and palpitating flesh intently enough to forget, as I can the make-believe of a fairy tale, that heavy drapery hanging from a cloud, though I find my pleasure in *King Lear* heightened by the make- believe that comes upon it all when the fool says: 'This prophecy Merlin shall make, for I live before his time';—and I always find it quite natural, so little does logic in the mere circumstance matter in the finest art, that Richard's and Richmond's tents should be side by side. I saw with delight *The Knight of the Burning Pestle* when Mr. Carr revived it, and found it none the worse because the apprentice acted a whole play upon the spur of the moment and without committing a line to heart. When Ben Jonson's *Epicœne* rammed a century of laughter into the two hours' traffic, I found with amazement that almost every journalist had put logic on the seat, where our lady imagination should pronounce that unjust and favouring sentence her woman's heart is ever plotting, and had felt bound to cherish none but reasonable sympathies and to resent the baiting of that grotesque old man. I have been looking over a book of engravings made in the eighteenth century from those wall-pictures of Herculaneum and Pompeii that were, it seems, the work of journeymen copying from finer paintings, for the composition is always too good for the execution. I find in great numbers an indifference to obvious logic, to all that the eye sees at common moments. Perseus shows Andromeda the death she lived by in a pool, and though the lovers are carefully drawn the reflection is upside down that we may see it the better. There is hardly an old master who has not made known to us in some like way how little he cares for what every fool can see and every knave can praise. The men who imagined the arts were not less superstitious in religion, understanding the spiritual relations, but not the mechanical, and finding nothing that need strain the throat in those gnats the floods of Noah and Deucalion, and in Joshua's moon at Ascalon.

CONCERNING SAINTS AND ARTISTS

I TOOK the Indian hemp with certain followers of St. Martin on the ground floor of a house in the Latin Quarter. I had never taken it before, and was instructed by a boisterous young poet, whose English was no better than my French. He gave me a little pellet, if I am not forgetting, an hour before dinner, and another after we had dined together at some restaurant. As we were going through the streets to the meeting-place of the Martinists, I felt suddenly that a cloud I was looking at floated in an immense space, and for an instant my being rushed out, as it seemed, into that space with ecstasy. I was myself again immediately, but the poet was wholly above himself, and presently he pointed to one of the street lamps now brightening in the fading twilight, and cried at the top of his voice, 'Why do you look at me with your great eye?' There were perhaps a dozen people already much excited when we arrived; and after I had drunk some cups of coffee and eaten a pellet or two more, I grew very anxious to dance, but did not, as I could not remember any steps. I sat down and closed my eyes; but no, I had no visions, nothing but a sensation of some dark shadow which seemed to be telling me that some day I would go into a trance and so out of my body for awhile, but not yet. I opened my eyes and looked at some red ornament on the mantelpiece, and at once the room was full of harmonies of red, but when a blue china figure caught my eye the harmonies became blue upon the instant. I was puzzled, for the reds were all there, nothing had changed, but they were no longer important or harmonious; and why had the blues so unimportant but a moment ago become exciting and delightful? Thereupon it struck me that I was seeing like a painter, and that in the course of the evening everyone there would change through every kind of artistic perception.

After a while a Martinist ran towards me with a piece of paper on which he had drawn a circle with a dot in it, and pointing at it with his finger he cried out, 'God, God!' Some immeasurable mystery had been revealed, and his eyes shone; and at some time or other a lean and shabby man, with rather a distinguished face, showed me his horoscope and pointed with an ecstasy of melancholy at its evil aspects. The boisterous poet, who was an old eater of the Indian hemp, had told me that it took one three months growing used to it, three months more enjoying it, and three months being cured of it. These men were in their second period; but I never forgot myself, never really rose above myself for more than a moment, and was even able to feel the absurdity of that gaiety, an Herr Nordau among the men of genius, but one that was abashed at his own sobriety. The sky outside was beginning to grey when there came a knocking at the window shutters. Somebody opened the window, and a woman in evening dress, who was not a little bewildered to find so many people, was helped down into the room. She had been at a students' ball unknown to her husband, who was asleep overhead, and had thought to have crept home unobserved, but for a confederate at the window. All those talking or dancing men laughed in a dreamy way; and she, understanding that there was no judgment in the laughter of men that had no thought but of the spectacle of the world, blushed, laughed and darted through the room and so upstairs. Alas that the hangman's rope should be own brother to that Indian happiness that keeps alone, were it not for some stray cactus, mother of as many dreams, an immemorial impartiality and simpleness.

THE SUBJECT MATTER OF DRAMA

I READ this sentence a few days ago, or one like it, in an obituary of Ibsen: 'Let nobody again go back to the old ballad material of Shakespeare, to murders, and ghosts, for what interests us on the stage is modern experience and the discussion of our interests'; and in another part of the article Ibsen was blamed because he had written of suicides and in other ways made use of 'the morbid terror of death.' Dramatic literature has for a long time been left to the criticism of journalists, and all these, the old stupid ones and the new clever ones, have tried to impress upon it their absorption in the life of the moment, their delight in obvious originality and in obvious logic, their shrinking from the ancient and insoluble. The writer I have quoted is much more than a journalist, but he has lived their hurried life, and instinctively turns to them for judgment. He is not thinking of the great poets and painters, of the cloud of witnesses, who are there that we may become, through our understanding of their minds, spectators of the ages, but of this age. Drama is a means of expression, not a special subject matter, and the dramatist is as free to choose where he has a mind to as the poet of 'Endymion' or as the painter of Mary Magdalene at the door of Simon the Pharisee. So far from the discussion of our interests and the immediate circumstance of our life being the most moving to the imagination, it is what is old and far off that stirs us the most deeply. There is a sentence in *The Marriage of Heaven and Hell* that is meaningless until we understand Blake's system of correspondences. 'The best wine is the oldest, the best water the newest.'

Water is experience, immediate sensation, and wine is emotion, and it is with the intellect, as distinguished from imagination, that we enlarge the bounds of experience and separate it from all but itself, from illusion, from memory, and create among other things science and good journalism. Emotion, on the other hand, grows intoxicating and delightful after it has been enriched with the memory of old emotions, with all the uncounted flavours of old experience, and it is necessarily an antiquity of thought, emotions that have been deepened by the experiences of many men of genius, that distinguishes the cultivated man. The subject-matter of his meditation and invention is old, and he will disdain a too conscious originality in the arts as in those matters of daily life where, is it not Balzac who says, 'we are all conservatives'? He is above all things well-bred, and whether he write or paint will not desire a technique that denies or obtrudes his long and noble descent. Corneille and Racine did not deny their masters, and when Dante spoke of his master Virgil there was no crowing of the cock. In their day imitation was conscious or all but conscious, and while originality was but so much the more a part of the man himself, so much the deeper because unconscious, no quick analysis could find out their miracle, that needed, it may be, generations to reveal; but it is our imitation that is unconscious and that waits the certainties of time. The more religious the subject-matter of an art, the more will it be as it were stationary, and the more ancient will be the emotion that it arouses and the circumstances that it calls up before our eyes. When in the Middle Ages the pilgrim to St. Patrick's Purgatory found himself on the lake side, he found a boat made out of a hollow tree to ferry him to the cave of vision. In religious painting and poetry, crowns and swords of an ancient pattern take upon themselves new meanings, and it is impossible to separate our idea of what is noble from a mystic stair, where not men and women, but robes, jewels, incidents, ancient utilities float upward slowly over the all but sleeping mind, putting on emotional and spiritual life as they ascend until they are swallowed up by some far glory that they even were too modern and momentary to endure. All art is dream, and what the day is done with is dreaming ripe, and what art moulds religion accepts, and in the end all is in the wine cup, all is in the drunken phantasy, and the grapes begin to stammer.

THE TWO KINDS OF ASCETICISM

I_T is not possible to separate an emotion or a spiritual state from the image that calls it up and gives it expression. Michael Angelo's Moses, Velasquez' Philip the Second, the colour purple, a crucifix, call into life an emotion or state that vanishes with them because they are its only possible expression, and that is why no mind is more valuable than the images it contains. The imaginative writer differs from the saint in that he identifies himself—to the neglect of his own soul, alas!—with the soul of the world, and frees himself from all that is impermanent in that soul, an ascetic not of women and wine, but of the newspapers. That which is permanent in the soul of the world upon the other hand, the great passions that trouble all and have but a brief recurring life of flower and seed in any man, is the renunciation of the saint who seeks not an eternal art, but his own eternity. The artist stands between the saint and the world of impermanent things, and just in so far as his mind dwells on what is impermanent in his sense, on all that 'modern experience and the discussion of our interests,' that is to say on what never recurs, as desire and hope, terror and weariness, spring and autumn, recur in varying rhythms, will his mind become critical, as distinguished from creative, and his emotions wither. He will think less of what he sees and more of his own attitude towards it, and will express this attitude by an essentially critical selection and emphasis. I am not quite sure of my memory, but I think that Mr. Ricketts has said in his book on the Prado that he feels the critic in Velasquez for the first time in painting, and we all feel the critic in Whistler and Degas, in Browning, even in Mr. Swinburne, in the finest art of all ages but the greatest. The end for art is the ecstasy awakened by the presence before an ever-changing mind of what is permanent in the world, or by the arousing of that mind itself into the very delicate and fastidious mood habitual with it when it is seeking those permanent and recurring things. There is a little of both ecstasies at all times, but at this time we have a small measure of the creative impulse itself, of the divine vision, a great one of 'the lost traveller's dream under the hill,' perhaps because all the old simple things have been painted or written, and they will only have meaning for us again when a new race or a new civilisation has made us look upon all with new eyesight.

IN THE SERPENT'S MOUTH

THERE is an old saying that God is a circle whose centre is everywhere. If that is true, the saint goes to the centre, the poet and artist to the ring where everything comes round again. The poet must not seek for what is still and fixed, for that has no life for him; and if he did, his style would become cold and monotonous, and his sense of beauty faint and sickly, as are both style and beauty to my imagination in the prose and poetry of Newman, but be content to find his pleasure in all that is for ever passing away that it may come again, in the beauty of woman, in the fragile flowers of spring, in momentary heroic passion, in whatever is most fleeting, most impassioned, as it were, for its own perfection, most eager to return in its glory. Yet perhaps he must endure the impermanent a little, for these things return, but not wholly, for no two faces are alike, and, it may be, had we more learned eyes, no two flowers. Is it that all things are made by the struggle of the individual and the world, of the unchanging and the returning, and that the saint and the poet are over all, and that the poet has made his home in the Serpent's mouth?

THE BLACK AND THE WHITE ARROWS

INSTINCT creates the recurring and the beautiful, all the winding of the serpent; but reason, the most ugly man, as Blake called it, is a drawer of the straight line, the maker of the arbitrary and the impermanent, for no recurring spring will ever bring again yesterday's clock. Sanctity has its straight line also, darting from the centre, and with these arrows the many-coloured serpent, theme of all our poetry, is maimed and hunted. He that finds the white arrow shall have wisdom older than the Serpent, but what of the black arrow? How much knowledge, how heavy a quiver of the crow-feathered ebony rods can the soul endure?

HIS MISTRESS'S EYEBROWS

THE preoccupation of our Art and Literature with knowledge, with the surface of life, with the arbitrary, with mechanism, has arisen out of the root. A careful, but not necessarily very subtle man, could foretell the history of any religion if he knew its first principle, and that it would live long enough to fulfil itself. The mind can never do the same thing twice over, and having exhausted simple beauty and meaning, it passes to the strange and hidden, and at last must find its delight, having outrun its harmonies in the emphatic and discordant. When I was a boy at the art school I watched an older student late returned from Paris, with a wonder that had no understanding in it. He was very amorous, and every new love was the occasion of a new picture, and every new picture was uglier than its forerunner. He was excited about his mistress's eyebrows, as was fitting, but the interest of beauty had been exhausted by the logical energies of Art, which destroys where it has rummaged, and can but discover, whether it will or no. We cannot discover our subject-matter by deliberate intellect, for when a subject-matter ceases to move us we must go elsewhere, and when it moves us, even though it be 'that old ballad material of Shakespeare' or even 'the morbid terror of death,' we can laugh at reason. We must not ask is the world interested in this or that, for nothing is in question but our own interest, and we can understand no other. Our place in the Hierarchy is settled for us by our choice of a subject-matter, and all good criticism is hieratic, delighting in setting things above one another, Epic and Drama above Lyric and so on, and not merely side by side. But it is our instinct and not our intellect that chooses. We can deliberately refashion our characters, but not our painting or our poetry. If our characters also were not unconsciously refashioned so completely by the unfolding of the logical energies of Art, that even simple things have in the end a new aspect in our eyes, the Arts would not be among those things that return for ever. The ballads that Bishop Percy gathered returned in the *Ancient Mariner* and the delight in the world of old Greek sculptors sprang into a more delicate loveliness in that archaistic head of the young athlete down the long corridor to your left hand as you go into the British Museum. Civilisation too, will not that also destroy where it has loved, until it shall bring the simple and natural things again and a new Argo with all the gilding on her bows sail out to find another fleece?

THE TRESSES OF THE HAIR

HAFIZ cried to his beloved, 'I made a bargain with that brown hair before the beginning of time, and it shall not be broken through unending time,' and it may be that Mistress Nature knows that we have lived many times, and that whatsoever changes and winds into itself belongs to us. She covers her eyes away from us, but she lets us play with the tresses of her hair.

A TOWER ON THE APENNINE

The other day I was walking towards Urbino, where I was to spend the night, having crossed the Apennines from San Sepolcro, and had come to a level place on the mountain-top near the journey's end. My friends were in a carriage somewhere behind, on a road which was still ascending in great loops, and I was alone amid a visionary fantastic impossible scenery. It was sunset and the stormy clouds hung upon mountain after mountain, and far off on one great summit a cloud darker than the rest glimmered with lightning. Away south upon another mountain a mediæval tower, with no building near nor any sign of life, rose into the clouds. I saw suddenly in the mind's eye an old man, erect and a little gaunt, standing in the door of the tower, while about him broke a windy light. He was the poet who had at last, because he had done so much for the world's sake, come to share in the dignity of the saint. He had hidden nothing of himself, but he had taken care of 'that dignity … the perfection of form … this lofty and severe quality … this virtue.' And though he had but sought it for the world's sake, or for a woman's praise, it had come at last into his body and his mind. Certainly as he stood there he knew how from behind that laborious mood, that pose, that genius, no flower of himself but all himself, looked out as from behind a mask that other Who alone of all men, the country people say, is not a hair's breadth more nor less than six feet high. He has in his ears well instructed voices and seeming solid sights are before his eyes, and not as we say of many a one, speaking in metaphor, but as this were Delphi or Eleusis, and the substance and the voice come to him among his memories which are of women's faces; for was it Columbanus or another that wrote 'There is one among the birds that is perfect, and one perfect among the fish'?

THE THINKING OF THE BODY

T_{HOSE} learned men who are a terror to children and an ignominious sight in lovers' eyes, all those butts of a traditional humour where there is something of the wisdom of peasants, are mathematicians, theologians, lawyers, men of science of various kinds. They have followed some abstract reverie, which stirs the brain only and needs that only, and have therefore stood before the looking-glass without pleasure and never known those thoughts that shape the lines of the body for beauty or animation, and wake a desire for praise or for display.

There are two pictures of Venice side by side in the house where I am writing this, a Canaletto that has little but careful drawing, and a not very emotional pleasure in clean bright air, and a Franz Francken, where the blue water, that in the other stirs one so little, can make one long to plunge into the green depth where a cloud shadow falls. Neither painting could move us at all, if our thought did not rush out to the edges of our flesh, and it is so with all good art, whether the Victory of Samothrace which reminds the soles of our feet of swiftness, or the Odyssey that would send us out under the salt wind, or the young horsemen on the Parthenon, that seem happier than our boyhood ever was, and in our boyhood's way. Art bids us touch and taste and hear and see the world, and shrinks from what Blake calls mathematic form, from every abstract thing, from all that is of the brain only, from all that is not a fountain jetting from the entire hopes, memories, and sensations of the body. Its morality is personal, knows little of any general law, has no blame for Little Musgrave, no care for Lord Barnard's house, seems lighter than a breath and yet is hard and heavy, for if a man is not ready to face toil and risk, and in all gaiety of heart, his body will grow unshapely and his heart lack the wild will that stirs desire. It approved before all men those that talked or wrestled or tilted under the walls of Urbino, or sat in the wide window-seats discussing all things, with love ever in their thought, when the wise Duchess ordered all, and the Lady Emilia gave the theme.

RELIGIOUS BELIEF NECESSARY TO SYMBOLIC ART

ALL art is sensuous, but when a man puts only his contemplative nature, and his more vague desires into his art, the sensuous images through which it speaks become broken, fleeting, uncertain, or are chosen for their distance from general experience, and all grows unsubstantial and fantastic. When imagination moves in a dim world like the country of sleep in 'Love's Nocturne' and 'Siren there winds her dizzy hair and sings' we go to it for delight indeed but in our weariness. If we are to sojourn there that world must grow consistent with itself, emotion must be related to emotion by a system of ordered images, as in the *Divine Comedy*. It must grow to be symbolic, that is, for the soul can only achieve a distinct separated life where many related objects at once distinguish and arouse its energies in their fulness. All visionaries have entered into such a world in trances, and all ideal art has trance for warranty. Shelley seemed to Matthew Arnold to beat his ineffectual wings in the void, and I only made my pleasure in him contented pleasure by massing in my imagination his recurring images of towers and rivers, and caves with fountains in them, and that one star of his, till his world had grown solid underfoot and consistent enough for the soul's habitation.

But even then I lacked something to compensate my imagination for geographical and historical reality, for the testimony of our ordinary senses, and found myself wishing for and trying to imagine, as I had also when reading Keats' *Endymion*, a crowd of believers who could put into all those strange sights the strength of their belief and the rare testimony of their visions. A little crowd had been sufficient, and I would have had Shelley a sectary that his revelation might have found the only sufficient evidence of religion, miracle. All symbolic art should arise out of a real belief, and that it cannot do so in this age proves that this age is a road and not a resting-place for the imaginative arts. I can only understand others by myself, and I am certain that there are many who are not moved as they desire to be by that solitary light burning in the tower of Prince Athanais, because it has not entered into men's prayers nor lighted any through the sacred dark of religious contemplation.

Lyrical poems even when they but speak of emotions common to all need, if not a religious belief like the spiritual arts, a life that has leisure for itself, and a society that is quickly stirred that our emotion may be strengthened by the emotion of others. All circumstance that makes emotion at once dignified and visible, increases the poet's power, and I think that is why I have always longed for some stringed instrument and a listening audience not drawn out of the hurried streets but from a life where it would be natural to murmur over again the singer's thought. When I heard Yvette Guilbert the other day, who has the lyre or as good, I was not content, for she sang among people whose life had nothing it could share with an exquisite art that should rise out of life as the blade out of the spearshaft, a song out of the mood, the fountain from its pool, all art out of the body, laughter from a happy company. I longed to make all things over again, that she might sing in some great hall, where there was no one that did not love life and speak of it continually.

THE HOLY PLACES

W<small>HEN</small> all art was struck out of personality, whether as in our daily business or in the adventure of religion, there was little separation between holy and common things, and just as the arts themselves passed quickly from passion to divine contemplation, from the conversation of peasants to that of princes, the one song remembering the drunken miller and but half forgetting Cambynskan bold; so did a man feel himself near sacred presences when he turned his plough from the slope of Cruachmaa or of Olympus. The occupations and the places known to Homer or to Hesiod, those pure first artists, might, as it were, if but the fashioners' hands had loosened, have changed before the poem's end to symbols and vanished, winged and unweary, into the unchanging worlds where religion only can discover life as well as peace. A man of that unbroken day could have all the subtlety of Shelley, and yet use no image unknown among the common people, and speak no thought that was not a deduction from the common thought. Unless the discovery of legendary knowledge and the returning belief in miracle, or what we must needs call so, can bring once more a new belief in the sanctity of common ploughland, and new wonders that reward no difficult ecclesiastical routine but the common, wayward, spirited man, we may never see again a Shelley and a Dickens in the one body, but be broken to the end. We have grown jealous of the body, and we dress it in dull unshapely clothes, that we may cherish aspiration alone. Molière being but the master of common sense lived ever in the common daylight, but Shakespeare could not, and Shakespeare seems to bring us to the very market-place, when we remember Shelley's dizzy and Landor's calm disdain of usual daily things. And at last we have Villiers de L'Isle Adam crying in the ecstasy of a supreme culture, of a supreme refusal, 'as for living, our servants will do that for us.' One of the means of loftiness, of marmorean stillness has been the choice of strange and far away places, for the scenery of art, but this choice has grown bitter to me, and there are moments when I cannot believe in the reality of imaginations that are not inset with the minute life of long familiar things and symbols and places. I have come to think of even Shakespeare's journeys to Rome or to Verona as the outflowing of an unrest, a dissatisfaction with natural interests, an unstable equilibrium of the whole European mind that would not have come had Constantinople wall been built of better stone. I am orthodox and pray for a resurrection of the body, and am certain that a man should find his Holy Land where he first crept upon the floor, and that familiar woods and rivers should fade into symbol with so gradual a change that he never discover, no, not even in ecstasy itself, that he is beyond space, and that time alone keeps him from Primum Mobile, the

Supernal Eden, and the White Rose over all.

EDMUND SPENSER

Included by kind permission of Messrs. T. C. and E. C. Jack.

I

W_E know little of Spenser's childhood and nothing of his parents, except that his father was probably an Edmund Spenser of north-east Lancashire, a man of good blood and 'belonging to a house of ancient fame.' He was born in London in 1552, nineteen years after the death of Ariosto, and when Tasso was about eight years old. Full of the spirit of the Renaissance, at once passionate and artificial, looking out upon the world now as craftsman, now as connoisseur, he was to found his art upon theirs rather than upon the more humane, the more noble, the less intellectual art of Malory and the Minstrels. Deafened and blinded by their influence, as so many of us were in boyhood by that art of Hugo, that made the old simple writers seem but as brown bread and water, he was always to love the journey more than its end, the landscape more than the man, and reason more than life, and the tale less than its telling. He entered Pembroke College, Cambridge, in 1569, and translated allegorical poems out of Petrarch and Du Bellay. To-day a young man translates out of Verlaine and Verhaeren; but at that day Ronsard and Du Bellay were the living poets, who promised revolutionary and unheard-of things to a poetry moving towards elaboration and intellect, as ours—the serpent's tooth in his own tail again—moves towards simplicity and instinct. At Cambridge he met with Hobbinol of *The Shepheards Calender*, a certain Gabriel Harvey, son of a rope-maker at Saffron Walden, but now a Fellow of Pembroke College, a notable man, some five or six years his elder. It is usual to think ill of Harvey, because of his dislike of rhyme and his advocacy of classical metres, and because he complained that Spenser preferred his *Faerie Queene* to the *Nine Muses*, and encouraged Hobgoblin 'to run off with the Garland of Apollo.' But at that crossroad, where so many crowds mingled talking of so many lands, no one could foretell in what bed he would sleep after nightfall. Milton was in the end to dislike rhyme as much, and it is certain that rhyme is one of the secondary causes of that disintegration of the personal instincts which has given to modern poetry its deep colour for colour's sake, its overflowing pattern, its background of decorative landscape, and its insubordination of detail. At the opening of a movement we are busy with first principles, and can find out everything but the road we are to go, everything but the weight and measure of the impulse, that has come to us out of life itself, for that is always in defiance of reason, always without a justification but by faith and works. Harvey set Spenser to the making of verses in classical metre, and certain lines have come down to us written in what Spenser called 'Iambicum trimetrum.' His biographers agree that they are very bad, but, though I cannot scan them, I find in them the charm of what seems a sincere personal emotion. The man himself, liberated from the minute felicities of phrase and sound, that are the temptation and the delight of rhyme, speaks of his Mistress some thought that came to him not for the sake of poetry, but for love's sake, and the emotion instead of dissolving into detached colours, into 'the spangly gloom' that Keats saw 'froth and boil' when he put his eyes into 'the pillowy cleft,' speaks to her in poignant words as if out of a tear-stained love-letter:

> 'Unhappie verse, the witnesse of my unhappie state,
>
> Make thy selfe fluttring winge for thy fast flying
>
> Thought, and fly forth to my love wheresoever she be.
>
> Whether lying restlesse in heavy bedde, or else
>
> Sitting so cheerlesse at the cheerful boorde, or else
>
> Playing alone carelesse on her heavenlie virginals.
>
> If in bed, tell hir that my eyes can take no rest;
>
> If at boorde tell her that my mouth can eat no meate;
>
> If at her virginals, tell her that I can heare no mirth.'

II

He left College in his twenty-fourth year, and stayed for a while in Lancashire, where he had relations, and there fell in love with one he has written of in *The Shepheards Calender* as 'Rosalind, the widdowes daughter of the Glenn,' though she was, for all her shepherding, as one learns from a College friend, 'a gentlewoman of no mean house.' She married Menalchus of the *Calender* and Spenser lamented her for years, in verses so full of disguise that one cannot say if his lamentations come out of a broken heart or are but a useful movement in the elaborate ritual of his poetry, a well-ordered incident in the mythology of his imagination. To no English poet, perhaps to no European poet before his day, had the natural expression of personal feeling been so impossible, the clear vision of the lineaments of human character so difficult; no other's head and eyes had sunk so far into the pillowy cleft. After a year of this life he went to London, and by Harvey's advice and introduction entered the service of the Earl of Leicester, staying for a while in his house on the banks of the Thames; and it was there in all likelihood that he met with the Earl's nephew, Sir Philip Sidney, still little more than a boy, but with his head full of affairs of state. One can imagine that it was the great Earl or Sir Philip Sidney that gave his imagination its moral and practical turn, and one imagines him seeking from philosophical men, who distrust instinct because it disturbs contemplation, and from practical men who distrust everything they cannot use in the routine of immediate events, that impulse and method of creation that can only be learned with surety from the technical criticism of poets, and from the excitement of some movement in the artistic life. Marlowe and Shakespeare were still at school, and Ben Jonson was but five years old. Sidney was doubtless the greatest personal influence that came into Spenser's life, and it was one that exalted moral zeal above every other faculty. The great Earl impressed his imagination very deeply also, for the lamentation over the Earl of Leicester's death is more than a conventional Ode to a dead patron. Spenser's verses about men, nearly always indeed, seem to express more of personal joy and sorrow than those about women, perhaps because he was less deliberately a poet when he spoke of men. At the end of a long beautiful passage he laments that unworthy men should be in the dead Earl's place, and compares them to the fox—an unclean feeder— hiding in the lair 'the badger swept.' The imaginer of the festivals of Kenilworth was indeed the fit patron for him, and alike, because of the strength and weakness of Spenser's art, one regrets that he could not have lived always in that elaborate life a master of ceremony to the world, instead of being plunged into a life that but stirred him to bitterness, as the way is with theoretical minds in the tumults of events they cannot understand. In the winter of 1579-80 he published *The Shepheards Calender*, a book of twelve eclogues, one for every month of the year, and dedicated it to Sir Philip Sidney. It was full of pastoral beauty and allegorical images of current events, revealing too that conflict between the æsthetic and moral interests that was to run through well-nigh all his works, and it became immediately famous. He was rewarded with a place as private secretary to the Lord Lieutenant, Lord Grey de Wilton, and sent to Ireland, where he spent nearly all the rest of his life. After a few years there he bought Kilcolman Castle, which had belonged to the rebel Earl of Desmond, and the rivers and hills about this castle came much into his poetry. Our Irish Aubeg is 'Mulla mine, whose waves I taught to weep,' and the Ballyvaughan Hills, it has its rise among, 'old Father Mole.' He never pictured the true countenance of Irish scenery, for his mind turned constantly to the courts of Elizabeth and to the umbrageous level lands, where his own race was already seeding like a great poppy:

'Both heaven and heavenly graces do much more
(Quoth he), abound in that same land then this:
For there all happie peace and plenteous store
Conspire in one to make contentedblisse.
No wayling there nor wretchednesse is heard,
No bloodie issues nor no leprosies,
No griesly famine, nor no raging sweard,

No nightly bordrags, nor no hue and cries;

The shepheards there abroad may safely lie

On hills and downes, withouten dread or daunger,

No ravenous wolves the good mans hope destroy,

Nor outlawes fell affray the forest raunger,

The learned arts do florish in great honor,

And Poets wits are had in peerlesse price.'

Nor did he ever understand the people he lived among or the historical events that were changing all things about him. Lord Grey de Wilton had been recalled almost immediately, but it was his policy, brought over ready-made in his ship, that Spenser advocated throughout all his life, equally in his long prose book *The State of Ireland* as in the *Faerie Queene*, where Lord Grey was Artigall and the Iron man the soldiers and executioners by whose hands he worked. Like an hysterical patient he drew a complicated web of inhuman logic out of the bowels of an insufficient premise—there was no right, no law, but that of Elizabeth, and all that opposed her opposed themselves to God, to civilisation, and to all inherited wisdom and courtesy, and should be put to death. He made two visits to England, celebrating one of them in *Colin Clouts come Home againe*, to publish the first three books and the second three books of the *Faerie Queene* respectively, and to try for some English office or pension. By the help of Raleigh, now his neighbour at Kilcolman, he had been promised a pension, but was kept out of it by Lord Burleigh, who said, 'All that for a song!' From that day Lord Burleigh became that 'rugged forehead' of the poems, whose censure of this or that is complained of. During the last three or four years of his life in Ireland he married a fair woman of his neighbourhood, and about her wrote many intolerable artificial sonnets and that most beautiful passage in the sixth book of the *Faerie Queene*, which tells of Colin Clout piping to the Graces and to her; and he celebrated his marriage in the most beautiful of all his poems, the *Epithalamium*. His genius was pictorial, and these pictures of happiness were more natural to it than any personal pride, or joy, or sorrow. His new happiness was very brief, and just as he was rising to something of Milton's grandeur in the fragment that has been called *Mutabilitie*, 'the wandering companies that keep the woods,' as he called the Irish armies, drove him to his death. Ireland, where he saw nothing but work for the Iron man, was in the midst of the last struggle of the old Celtic order with England, itself about to turn bottom upward, of the passion of the Middle Ages with the craft of the Renaissance. Seven years after Spenser's arrival in Ireland a large merchant ship had carried off from Loch Swilly, by a very crafty device common in those days, certain persons of importance. Red Hugh, a boy of fifteen, and the coming head of Tirconnell, and various heads of clans had been enticed on board the merchant ship to drink of a fine vintage, and there made prisoners. All but Red Hugh were released, on finding substitutes among the boys of their kindred, and the captives were hurried to Dublin and imprisoned in the Burningham Tower. After four years of captivity and one attempt that failed, Red Hugh and his companions escaped into the Dublin mountains, one dying there of cold and privation, and from that to their own country-side. Red Hugh allied himself to Hugh O'Neil, the most powerful of the Irish leaders—'Oh, deep, dissembling heart, born to great weal or woe of thy country!' an English historian had cried to him—an Oxford man too, a man of the Renaissance, and for a few years defeated English armies and shook the power of England. The Irish, stirred by these events, and with it maybe some rumours of *The State of Ireland* sticking in their stomachs, drove Spenser out of doors and burnt his house, one of his children, as tradition has it, dying in the fire. He fled to England, and died some three months later in January, 1599, as Ben Jonson says, 'of lack of bread.'

During the last four or five years of his life he had seen, without knowing that he saw it, the beginning of the great Elizabethan poetical movement. In 1598 he had pictured the Nine Muses lamenting each one over the evil state in England, of the things that she had in charge, but, like William Blake's more beautiful *Whether on Ida's shady brow*, their lamentations should have been a cradle-song. When he died *Romeo and Juliet, Richard III.*, and *Richard II.*, and the plays of Marlowe had all been acted, and in stately houses were sung madrigals and love songs whose like has not been in the world since. Italian influence had strengthened the old French joy that had never died out among the upper classes, and an art was being created for the last time in England which had half its beauty from continually suggesting a life hardly less beautiful than itself.

III

When Spenser was buried at Westminster Abbey many poets read verses in his praise, and threw then their verses and the pens that had written them into his tomb. Like him they belonged, for all the moral zeal that was gathering like a London fog, to that indolent, demonstrative Merry England that was about to pass away. Men still wept when they were moved, still dressed themselves in joyous colours, and spoke with many gestures. Thoughts and qualities sometimes come to their perfect expression when they are about to pass away, and Merry England was dying in plays, and in poems, and in strange adventurous men. If one of those poets who threw his copy of verses into the earth that was about to close over his master were to come alive again, he would find some shadow of the life he knew, though not the art he knew, among young men in Paris, and would think that his true country. If he came to England he would find nothing there but the triumph of the Puritan and the merchant—those enemies he had feared and hated—and he would weep perhaps, in that womanish way of his, to think that so much greatness had been, not as he had hoped, the dawn, but the sunset of a people. He had lived in the last days of what we may call the Anglo-French nation, the old feudal nation that had been established when the Norman and the Angevin made French the language of court and market. In the time of Chaucer English poets still wrote much in French, and even English labourers lilted French songs over their work; and I cannot read any Elizabethan poem or romance without feeling the pressure of habits of emotion, and of an order of life which were conscious, for all their Latin gaiety, of a quarrel to the death with that new Anglo-Saxon nation that was arising amid Puritan sermons and Mar-Prelate pamphlets. This nation had driven out the language of its conquerors, and now it was to overthrow their beautiful, haughty imagination and their manners, full of abandon and wilfulness, and to set in their stead earnestness and logic and the timidity and reserve of a counting-house. It had been coming for a long while, for it had made the Lollards; and when Anglo- French Chaucer was at Westminster its poet, Langland, sang the office at St. Paul's. Shakespeare, with his delight in great persons, with his indifference to the State, with his scorn of the crowd, with his feudal passion, was of the old nation, and Spenser, though a joyless earnestness had cast shadows upon him, and darkened his intellect wholly at times, was of the old nation too. His *Faerie Queene* was written in Merry England, but when Bunyan wrote in prison the other great English allegory Modern England had been born. Bunyan's men would do right that they might come some day to the Delectable Mountain, and not at all that they might live happily in a world whose beauty was but an entanglement about their feet. Religion had denied the sacredness of an earth that commerce was about to corrupt and ravish, but when Spenser lived the earth had still its sheltering sacredness. His religion, where the paganism that is natural to proud and happy people had been strengthened by the platonism of the Renaissance, cherished the beauty of the soul and the beauty of the body with, as it seemed, an equal affection. He would have had men live well, not merely that they might win eternal happiness but that they might live splendidly among men and be celebrated in many songs. How could one live well if one had not the joy of the Creator and of the Giver of gifts? He says in his *Hymn to Beauty* that a beautiful soul, unless for some stubbornness in the ground, makes for itself a beautiful body, and he even denies that beautiful persons ever lived who had not souls as beautiful. They may have been tempted until they seemed evil, but that was the fault of others. And in his *Hymn to Heavenly Beauty* he sets a woman little known to theology, one that he names Wisdom or Beauty, above

Seraphim and Cherubim and in the very bosom of God, and in the *Faerie Queene* it is pagan Venus and her lover Adonis who create the forms of all living things and send them out into the world, calling them back again to the gardens of Adonis at their lives' end to rest there, as it seems, two thousand years between life and life. He began in English poetry, despite a temperament that delighted in sensuous beauty alone with perfect delight, that worship of Intellectual Beauty which Shelley carried to a much greater subtlety and applied to the whole of life.

The qualities, to each of whom he had planned to give a Knight, he had borrowed from Aristotle and partly Christianised, but not to the forgetting of their heathen birth. The chief of the Knights, who would have combined in himself the qualities of all the others, had Spenser lived to finish the *Faerie Queene*, was King Arthur, the representative of an ancient quality, Magnificence. Born at the moment of change, Spenser had indeed many Puritan thoughts. It has been recorded that he cut his hair short and half regretted his hymns to Love and Beauty. But he has himself told us that the many-headed beast overthrown and bound by Calidor, Knight of Courtesy, was Puritanism itself. Puritanism, its zeal and its narrowness, and the angry suspicion that it had in common with all movements of the ill-educated, seemed no other to him than a slanderer of all fine things. One doubts, indeed, if he could have persuaded himself that there could be any virtue at all without courtesy, perhaps without something of pageant and eloquence. He was, I think, by nature altogether a man of that old Catholic feudal nation, but, like Sidney, he wanted to justify himself to his new masters. He wrote of knights and ladies, wild creatures imagined by the aristocratic poets of the twelfth century, and perhaps chiefly by English poets who had still the French tongue; but he fastened them with allegorical nails to a big barn door of common-sense, of merely practical virtue. Allegory itself had risen into general importance with the rise of the merchant class in the thirteenth and fourteenth centuries; and it was natural when that class was about for the first time to shape an age in its image, that the last epic poet of the old order should mix its art with his own long-descended, irresponsible, happy art.

IV

Allegory and, to a much greater degree, symbolism are a natural language by which the soul when entranced, or even in ordinary sleep, communes with God and with angels. They can speak of things which cannot be spoken of in any other language, but one will always, I think, feel some sense of unreality when they are used to describe things which can be described as well in ordinary words. Dante used allegory to describe visionary things, and the first

41

maker of *The Romance of the Rose*, for all his lighter spirits, pretends that his adventures came to him in a vision one May morning; while Bunyan, by his preoccupation with heaven and the soul, gives his simple story a visionary strangeness and intensity: he believes so little in the world, that he takes us away from all ordinary standards of probability and makes us believe even in allegory for a while. Spenser, on the other hand, to whom allegory was not, as I think, natural at all, makes us feel again and again that it disappoints and interrupts our preoccupation with the beautiful and sensuous life he has called up before our eyes. It interrupts us most when he copies Langland, and writes in what he believes to be a mood of edification, and the least when he is not quite serious, when he sets before us some procession like a court pageant made to celebrate a wedding or a crowning. One cannot think that he should have occupied himself with moral and religious questions at all. He should have been content to be, as Emerson thought Shakespeare was, a Master of the Revels to mankind. I am certain that he never gets that visionary air which can alone make allegory real, except when he writes out of a feeling for glory and passion. He had no deep moral or religious life. He has never a line like Dante's 'Thy Will is our Peace,' or like Thomas à Kempis's 'The Holy Spirit has liberated me from a multitude of opinions,' or even like Hamlet's objection to the bare bodkin. He had been made a poet by what he had almost learnt to call his sins. If he had not felt it necessary to justify his art to some serious friend, or perhaps even to 'that rugged forehead,' he would have written all his life long, one thinks, of the loves of shepherdesses and shepherds, among whom there would have been perhaps the morals of the dovecot. One is persuaded that his morality is official and impersonal—a system of life which it was his duty to support—and it is perhaps a half understanding of this that has made so many generations believe that he was the first poet laureate, the first salaried moralist among the poets. His processions of deadly sins, and his houses, where the very cornices are arbitrary images of virtue, are an unconscious hypocrisy, an undelighted obedience to the 'rugged forehead,' for all the while he is thinking of nothing but lovers whose bodies are quivering with the memory or the hope of long embraces. When they are not together, he will indeed embroider emblems and images much as those great ladies of the courts of love embroidered them in their castles; and when these are imagined out of a thirst for magnificence and not thought out in a mood of edification, they are beautiful enough; but they are always tapestries for corridors that lead to lovers' meetings or for the walls of marriage chambers. He was not passionate, for the passionate feed their flame in wanderings and absences, when the whole being of the beloved, every little charm of body and of soul, is always present to the mind, filling it with heroical subtleties of desire. He is a poet of the delighted senses, and his song becomes most beautiful when he writes of those islands of Phædria and

Acrasia, which angered 'that rugged forehead,' as it seems, but gave to Keats his *Belle Dame sans Merci* and his 'perilous seas in faery lands forlorn,' and to William Morris his *Water of the Wondrous Isles*.

V

The dramatists lived in a disorderly world, reproached by many, persecuted even, but following their imagination wherever it led them. Their imagination, driven hither and thither by beauty and sympathy, put on something of the nature of eternity. Their subject was always the soul, the whimsical, self-awakening, self-exciting, self-appeasing soul. They celebrated its heroical, passionate will going by its own path to immortal and invisible things. Spenser, on the other hand, except among those smooth pastoral scenes and lovely effeminate islands that have made him a great poet, tried to be of his time, or rather of the time that was all but at hand. Like Sidney, whose charm it may be led many into slavery, he persuaded himself that we enjoy Virgil because of the virtues of Æneas, and so planned out his immense poem that it would set before the imagination of citizens, in whom there would soon be no great energy, innumerable blameless Æneases. He had learned to put the State, which desires all the abundance for itself, in the place of the Church, and he found it possible to be moved by expedient emotions, merely because they were expedient, and to think serviceable thoughts with no self-contempt. He loved his Queen a little because she was the protectress of poets and an image of that old Anglo-French nation that lay a-dying, but a great deal because she was the image of the State which had taken possession of his conscience. She was over sixty years old, and ugly and, it is thought, selfish, but in his poetry she is 'fair Cynthia,' 'a crown of lilies,' 'the image of the heavens,' 'without mortal blemish,' and has 'an angelic face,' where 'the red rose' has 'meddled with the white'; 'Phœbus thrusts out his golden head' but to look upon her, and blushes to find himself outshone. She is 'a fourth Grace,' 'a queen of love,' 'a sacred saint,' and 'above all her sex that ever yet has been.' In the midst of his praise of his own sweetheart he stops to remember that Elizabeth is more beautiful, and an old man in *Daphnaida*, although he has been brought to death's door by the death of a beautiful daughter, remembers that though his daughter 'seemed of angelic race,' she was yet but the primrose to the rose beside Elizabeth. Spenser had learned to look to the State not only as the rewarder of virtue but as the maker of right and wrong, and had begun to love and hate as it bid him. The thoughts that we find for ourselves are timid and a little secret, but those modern thoughts that we share with large numbers are confident and very insolent. We have little else to-day, and when we read our newspaper and take up its cry, above all its cry of hatred, we will not think very carefully, for we hear the marching feet.

When Spenser wrote of Ireland he wrote as an official, and out of thoughts and emotions that had been organised by the State. He was the first of many Englishmen to see nothing but what he was desired to see. Could he have gone there as a poet merely, he might have found among its poets more wonderful imaginations than even those islands of Phædria and Acrasia. He would have found among wandering storytellers, not indeed his own power of rich, sustained description, for that belongs to lettered ease, but certainly all the kingdom of Faerie, still unfaded, of which his own poetry was often but a troubled image. He would have found men doing by swift strokes of the imagination much that he was doing with painful intellect, with that imaginative reason that soon was to drive out imagination altogether and for a long time. He would have met with, at his own door, storytellers among whom the perfection of Greek art was indeed as unknown as his own power of detailed description, but who, none the less, imagined or remembered beautiful incidents and strange, pathetic out-crying that made them of Homer's lineage. Flaubert says somewhere, 'There are things in Hugo, as in Rabelais, that I could have mended, things badly built, but then what thrusts of power beyond the reach of conscious art!' Is not all history but the coming of that conscious art which first makes articulate and then destroys the old wild energy? Spenser, the first poet struck with remorse, the first poet who gave his heart to the State, saw nothing but disorder, where the mouths that have spoken all the fables of the poets had not yet become silent. All about him were shepherds and shepherdesses still living the life that made Theocritus and Virgil think of shepherd and poet as the one thing; but though he dreamed of Virgil's shepherds he wrote a book to advise, among many like things, the harrying of all that followed flocks upon the hills, and of all 'the wandering companies that keep the woods.' His *View of the State of Ireland* commends indeed the beauty of the hills and woods where they did their shepherding, in that powerful and subtle language of his which I sometimes think more full of youthful energy than even the language of the great playwrights. He is 'sure it is yet a most beautiful and sweet country as any under heaven,' and that all would prosper but for those agitators, 'those wandering companies that keep the wood,' and he would rid it of them by a certain expeditious way. There should be four great garrisons. 'And those fowre garrisons issuing foorthe, at such convenient times as they shall have intelligence or espiall upon the enemye, will so drive him from one side to another and tennis him amongst them, that he shall finde nowhere safe to keepe his creete, or hide himselfe, but flying from the fire shall fall into the water, and out of one daunger into another, that in short space his creete, which is his moste sustenence, shall be wasted in preying, or killed in driving, or starved for wante of pasture in the woodes, and he himselfe brought soe lowe, that he shall have no harte nor abilitye to indure his wretchednesse, the which will surely come to passe in very short space; for one winters well following of him will so plucke him on his knees that he will never be able to stand up agayne.'

He could commend this expeditious way from personal knowledge, and could assure the Queen that the people of the country would soon 'consume themselves and devoure one another. The proofs whereof I saw sufficiently ensampled in these late warres of Mounster; for notwithstanding that the same was a most rich and plentifull countrey, full of corne and cattell, that you would have thought they would have bene able to stand long, yet ere one yeare and a halfe they were brought to such wretchednesse, as that any stonye heart would have rued the same. Out of every corner of the woodes and glynnes they came creeping forth upon theyr hands, for theyr legges could not beare them; they looked like anatomyes of death, they spake like ghosts crying out of their graves; they did eate of the dead carrions, happy were they if they could finde them, yea, and one another soone after, insomuch as the very carcasses they spared not to scrape out of theyr graves; and if they found a plot of water-cresses or shamrokes, there they flocked as to a feast for the time, yet not able long to continue therewithall; that in short space there were none allmost left, and a most populous and plentifull countrey suddaynely left voyde of man or beast; yet sure in all that warre, there perished not many by the sword, but all by the extremitye of famine.'

VI

In a few years the Four Masters were to write the history of that time, and they were to record the goodness or the badness of Irishman and Englishman with entire impartiality. They had seen friends and relatives persecuted, but they would write of that man's poisoning and this man's charities and of the fall of great houses, and hardly with any other emotion than a thought of the pitiableness of all life. Friend and enemy would be for them a part of the spectacle of the world. They remembered indeed those Anglo-French invaders who conquered for the sake of their own strong hand, and when they had conquered became a part of the life about them, singing its songs, when they grew weary of their own Iseult and Guinevere. But the Four Masters had not come to understand, as I think, despite famines and exterminations, that new invaders were among them, who fought for an alien State, for an alien religion. Such ideas were difficult to them, for they belonged to the old individual, poetical life, and spoke a language even in which it was all but impossible to think an abstract thought. They understood Spain, doubtless, which persecuted in the interests of religion, but I doubt if anybody in Ireland could have understood as yet that the Anglo-Saxon nation was beginning to persecute in the service of ideas it believed to be the foundation of the State. I doubt if anybody in Ireland saw that with certainty, till the Great Demagogue had come and turned the old house of the noble into 'the house of the Poor, the lonely house, the accursed house of Cromwell.' He came, another Cairbry Cat Head, with that great rabble, who had overthrown the pageantry of Church and Court, but who turned towards him faces full of the sadness and docility of their long servitude, and the old individual, poetical life went down, as it seems, for ever. He had studied Spenser's book and approved of it, as we know, finding, doubtless, his own head there, for Spenser, a king of the old race, carried a mirror which showed kings yet to come though but kings of the mob. Those Bohemian poets of the theatres were wiser, for the States that touched them nearly were the States where Helen and Dido had sorrowed, and so their mirrors showed none but beautiful heroical heads. They wandered in the places that pale passion loves, and were happy, as one thinks, and troubled little about those marching and hoarse-throated thoughts that the State has in its pay. They knew that those marchers, with the dust of so many roads upon them, are very robust and have great and well-paid generals to write expedient despatches in sound prose; and they could hear mother earth singing among her cornfields:

'Weep not, my wanton! smile upon my knee;

When thou art old there's grief enough for thee.'

VII

There are moments when one can read neither Milton nor Spenser, moments when one recollects nothing but that their flesh had partly been changed to stone, but there are other moments when one recollects nothing but those habits of emotion that made the lesser poet especially a man of an older, more imaginative time. One remembers that he delighted in smooth pastoral places, because men could be busy there or gather together there, after their work, that he could love handiwork and the hum of voices. One remembers that he could still rejoice in the trees, not because they were images of loneliness and meditation, but because of their serviceableness. He could praise 'the builder oake,' 'the aspine, good for staves,' 'the cypresse funerall,' 'the eugh, obedient to the bender's will,' 'the birch for shaftes,' 'the sallow for the mill,' 'the mirrhe sweete-bleeding in the bitter wound,' 'the fruitful olive,' and 'the carver holme.' He was of a time before undelighted labour had made the business of men a desecration. He carries one's memory back to Virgil's and Chaucer's praise of trees, and to the sweet-sounding song made by the old Irish poet in their praise.

I got up from reading the *Faerie Queene* the other day and wandered into another room. It was in a friend's house, and I came of a sudden to the ancient poetry and to our poetry side by side—an engraving of Claude's 'Mill' hung under an engraving of Turner's 'Temple of Jupiter.' Those dancing country people, those cow-herds, resting after the day's work, and that quiet mill-race made one think of Merry England with its glad Latin heart, of a time when men in every land found poetry and imagination in one another's company and in the day's labour. Those stately goddesses, moving in slow procession towards that marble architrave among mysterious trees, belong to Shelley's thought, and to the religion of the wilderness—the only religion possible to poetry to-day. Certainly Colin Clout, the companionable shepherd, and Calidor, the courtly man-at-arms, are gone, and Alastor is wandering from lonely river to river finding happiness in nothing but in that star where Spenser too had imagined the fountain of perfect things. This new beauty, in losing so much, has indeed found a new loftiness, a something of religious exaltation that the old had not. It may be that those goddesses, moving with a majesty like a procession of the stars, mean something to the soul of man that those kindly women of the old poets did not mean, for all the fulness of their breasts and the joyous gravity of their eyes. Has not the wilderness been at all times a place of prophecy?

VIII

Our poetry, though it has been a deliberate bringing back of the Latin joy and the Latin love of beauty, has had to put off the old marching rhythms, that once delighted more than expedient hearts, in separating itself from a life where servile hands have become powerful. It has ceased to have any burden for marching shoulders, since it learned ecstasy from Smart in his mad cell, and from Blake, who made joyous little songs out of almost unintelligible visions, and from Keats, who sang of a beauty so wholly preoccupied with itself that its contemplation is a kind of lingering trance. The poet, if he would not carry burdens that are not his and obey the orders of servile lips, must sit apart in contemplative indolence playing with fragile things.

If one chooses at hazard a Spenserian stanza out of Shelley and compares it with any stanza by Spenser, one sees the change, though it would be still more clear if one had chosen a lyrical passage. I will take a stanza out of *Laon and Cythna*, for that is story-telling and runs nearer to Spenser than the meditative *Adonais:*

'The meteor to its far morass returned:

The beating of our veins one interval

Made still; and then I felt the blood that burned

Within her frame, mingle with mine, and fall

Around my heart like fire; and over all

A mist was spread, the sickness of a deep

And speechless swoon of joy, as might befall

Two disunited spirits when they leap

In union from this earth's obscure and fading sleep.'

The rhythm is varied and troubled, and the lines, which are in Spenser like bars of gold thrown ringing one upon another, are broken capriciously. Nor is the meaning the less an inspiration of indolent muses, for it wanders hither and thither at the beckoning of fancy. It is now busy with a meteor and now with throbbing blood that is fire, and with a mist that is a swoon and a sleep that is life. It is bound together by the vaguest suggestion, while Spenser's verse is always rushing on to some preordained thought. 'A popular poet' can still indeed write poetry of the will, just as factory girls wear the fashion of hat or dress the moneyed classes wore a year ago, but 'popular poetry' does not belong to the living imagination of the world. Old writers gave men four temperaments, and they gave the sanguineous temperament to men of active life, and it is precisely the sanguineous temperament that is fading out of poetry and most obviously out of what is most subtle and living in poetry—its pulse and breath, its rhythm. Because poetry belongs to that element in every race which is most strong, and therefore most individual, the poet is not stirred to imaginative activity by a life which is surrendering its freedom to ever new elaboration, organisation, mechanism. He has no longer a poetical will, and must be content to write out of those parts of himself which are too delicate and fiery for any deadening exercise. Every generation has more and more loosened the rhythm, more and more broken up and disorganised, for the sake of subtlety or detail, those great rhythms which move, as it were, in masses of sound. Poetry has become more spiritual, for the soul is of all things the most delicately organised, but it has lost in weight and measure and in its power of telling long stories and of dealing with great and complicated events. *Laon and Cythna*, though I think it rises sometimes into loftier air than the *Faerie Queene*, and *Endymion*, though its shepherds and wandering divinities have a stranger and more intense beauty than Spenser's, have need of too watchful and minute attention for such lengthy poems. In William Morris, indeed, one finds a music smooth and unexacting like that of the old story-tellers, but not their energetic pleasure, their rhythmical wills. One too often misses in his *Earthly Paradise* the minute ecstasy of modern song without finding that old happy-go-lucky tune that had kept the story marching.

Spenser's contemporaries, writing lyrics or plays full of lyrical moments, write a verse more delicately organised than his and crowd more meaning into a phrase than he, but they could not have kept one's attention through so long a poem. A friend who has a fine ear told me the other day that she had read all Spenser with delight and yet could remember only four lines. When she repeated them they were from the poem by Matthew Roydon, which is bound up with Spenser because it is a commendation of Sir Philip Sidney:

'A sweet, attractive kind of grace,

A full assurance given by looks,

Continual comfort in a face,

The lineaments of Gospel books.'

Yet if one were to put even these lines beside a fine modern song one would notice that they had a stronger and rougher energy, a feather-weight more, if eye and ear were fine enough to notice it, of the active will, of the happiness that comes out of life itself.

IX

I have put into this book[A] only those passages from Spenser that I want to remember and carry about with me. I have not tried to select what people call characteristic passages, for that is, I think, the way to make a dull book. One never really knows anybody's taste but one's own, and if one likes anything sincerely one may be certain that there are other people made out of the same earth to like it too. I have taken out of *The Shepheards Calender* only those parts which are about love or about old age, and I have taken out of the *Faerie Queene* passages about shepherds and lovers, and fauns and satyrs, and a few allegorical processions. I find that though I love symbolism, which is often the only fitting speech for some mystery of disembodied life, I am for the most part bored by allegory, which is made, as Blake says, 'by the daughters of memory,' and coldly, with no wizard frenzy. The processions I have chosen are either those, like the House of Mammon, that have enough ancient mythology, always an implicit symbolism, or, like the Cave of Despair, enough sheer passion to make one forget or forgive their allegory, or else they are, like that vision of Scudamour, so visionary, so full of a sort of ghostly midnight animation, that one is persuaded that they had some strange purpose and did truly appear in just that way to some mind worn out with war and trouble. The vision of Scudamour is, I sometimes think, the finest invention in Spenser. Until quite lately I knew nothing of Spenser but the parts I had read as a boy. I did not know that I had read so far as that vision, but year after year this thought would rise up before me coming from I knew not where. I would be alone perhaps in some old building, and I would think suddenly 'out of that door might come a procession of strange people doing mysterious things with tumult. They would walk over the stone floor, then suddenly vanish, and everything would become silent again.' Once I saw what is called,

I think, a Board School continuation class play *Hamlet*. There was no stage, but they walked in procession into the midst of a large room full of visitors and of their friends. While they were walking in, that thought came to me again from I knew not where. I was alone in a great church watching ghostly kings and queens setting out upon their unearthly business.

It was only last summer, when I read the Fourth Book of the *Faerie Queene*, that I found I had been imagining over and over the enchanted persecution of Amoret.

I give too, in a section which I call 'Gardens of Delight,' the good gardens of Adonis and the bad gardens of Phædria and Acrasia, which are mythological and symbolical, but not allegorical, and show, more particularly those bad islands, his power of describing bodily happiness and bodily beauty at its greatest. He seemed always to feel through the eyes, imagining everything in pictures. Marlowe's *Hero and Leander* is more energetic in its sensuality, more complicated in its intellectual energy than this languid story, which pictures always a happiness that would perish if the desire to which it offers so many roses lost its indolence and its softness. There is no passion in the pleasure he has set amid perilous seas, for he would have us understand that there alone could the war-worn and the sea-worn man find date-less leisure and unrepining peace.

October, 1902.

POETRY AND TRADITION

I

W_{HEN} Mr. O'Leary died I could not bring myself to go to his funeral, though I had been once his close fellow-worker, for I shrank from seeing about his grave so many whose Nationalism was different from anything he had taught or that I could share. He belonged, as did his friend John F. Taylor, to the romantic conception of Irish Nationality on which Lionel Johnson and myself founded, so far as it was founded on anything but literature, our Art and our Irish criticism. Perhaps his spirit, if it can care for or can see old friends now, will accept this apology for an absence that has troubled me. I learned much from him and much from Taylor, who will always seem to me the greatest orator I have heard; and that ideal Ireland, perhaps from this out an imaginary Ireland, in whose service I labour, will always be in many essentials their Ireland. They were the last to speak an understanding of life and Nationality, built up by the generation of Grattan, which read Homer and Virgil, and by the generation of Davis, which had been pierced through by the idealism of Mazzini,[B] and of the European revolutionists of the mid-century.

O'Leary had joined the Fenian movement with no hope of success as we know, but because he believed such a movement good for the moral character of the people; and had taken his long imprisonment without complaining. Even to the very end, while often speaking of his prison life, he would have thought it took from his Roman courage to describe its hardship. The worth of a man's acts in the moral memory, a continual height of mind in the doing of them, seemed more to him than their immediate result, if, indeed, the sight of many failures had not taken away the thought of success. A man was not to lie, or even to give up his dignity, on any patriotic plea, and I have heard him say, 'I have but one religion, the old Persian: to bend the bow and tell the truth,' and again, 'There are things a man must not do to save a nation,' and again, 'A man must not cry in public to save a nation,' and that we might not forget justice in the passion of controversy. 'There was never cause so bad that it has not been defended by good men for what seemed to them good reasons.' His friend had a burning and brooding imagination that divided men not according to their achievement but by their degrees of sincerity, and by their mastery over a straight and, to my thought, too obvious logic that seemed to him essential to sincerity. Neither man had an understanding of style or of literature in the right sense of the word, though both were great readers, but because their imagination could come to rest no place short of greatness, they hoped, John O'Leary especially, for an Irish literature of the greatest kind. When Lionel Johnson and Katharine Tynan (as she was then), and I, myself, began to reform Irish poetry, we thought to keep unbroken the thread running up to Grattan which John O'Leary had put into our hands, though it might be our business to explore new paths of the labyrinth. We sought to make a more subtle rhythm, a more organic form, than that of the older Irish poets who wrote in English, but always to remember certain ardent ideas and high attitudes of mind which were the nation itself, to our belief, so far as a nation can be summarised in the intellect. If you had asked an ancient Spartan what made Sparta Sparta, he would have answered, The Laws of Lycurgus, and many Englishmen look back to Bunyan and to Milton as we did to Grattan and to Mitchell. Lionel Johnson was able to take up into his Art one portion of this tradition that I could not, for he had a gift of speaking political thought in fine verse that I have always lacked. I, on the other hand, was more preoccupied with Ireland (for he had other interests), and took from Allingham and Walsh their passion for country spiritism, and from Ferguson his pleasure in heroic legend, and while seeing all in the light of European literature found my symbols of expression in Ireland. One thought often possessed me very strongly. New from the influence, mainly the personal influence, of William Morris, I dreamed of enlarging Irish hate, till we had come to hate with a passion of patriotism what Morris and Ruskin hated. Mitchell had already all but poured some of that hate drawn from Carlyle, who had it of an earlier and, as I think, cruder sort, into the blood of Ireland, and were we not a poor nation with ancient courage, unblackened fields, and a barbarous gift of self-sacrifice? Ruskin and Morris had spent themselves in vain because they had found no passion to harness to their thought, but here was unwasted passion and precedents in the popular memory for every needed thought and action. Perhaps, too, it would be possible to find in that new philosophy of spiritism coming to a seeming climax in the work of Ernest Myers, and in the investigations of uncounted obscure persons, what could change the country spiritism into a reasoned belief that would put its might into all the rest. A new belief seemed coming that could be so simple and demonstratable and above all so mixed into the common scenery of the world, that it would set the whole man on fire and liberate him from a thousand obediences and complexities. We were to forge in Ireland a new sword on our old traditional anvil for that great battle that must in the end re- establish the old, confident, joyous world. All the while I worked with this idea, founding societies that became quickly or slowly everything I despise. One part of me looked on, mischievous and mocking, and the other part spoke words which were more and more unreal, as the attitude of mind became more and more strained and difficult. Madame Maud Gonne could still draw great crowds out of the slums by her beauty and sincerity, and speak to them of 'Mother Ireland with the crown of stars about her head.' But gradually the political movement she was associated with, finding it hard to build up any fine lasting thing, became content to attack little persons and little things. All movements are held together more by what they hate than what they love, for love separates and individualises and quiets, but the nobler movements, the only movements on which literature can found itself, hate great and lasting things. All who have any old traditions, have something of aristocracy, but we had opposing us from the first, though not strongly from the first, a type of mind which had been without influence in the generation of Grattan, and almost without it in that of Davis, and which has made a new nation out of Ireland, that was once old and full of memories.

I remember, when I was twenty years old, arguing, on my way home from a Young Ireland Society, that Ireland, with its hieratic Church, its readiness to accept leadership in intellectual things—and John O'Leary spoke much of this readiness[C]—its Latin hatred of middle paths and uncompleted arguments, could never create a democratic poet of the type of Burns, although it had tried to do so more than once, but that its genius would in the long run be aristocratic and lonely. Whenever I had known some old countryman, I had heard stories and sayings that arose out of an imagination that would have understood Homer better than 'The Cotter's Saturday Night' or 'Highland Mary,' because it was an ancient imagination, where the sediment had found the time to settle, and I believed that the makers of deliberate literature could still take passion and theme, though but little thought, from such as he. On some such old and broken stem, I thought, have all the most beautiful roses been grafted.

II

Him who trembles before the flame and the flood,

And the winds that blow through the starry ways;

Let the starry winds and the flame and the flood

Cover over and hide, for he has no part

With the proud, majestical, multitude.

THREE types of men have made all beautiful things. Aristocracies have made beautiful manners, because their place in the world puts them above the fear of life, and the countrymen have made beautiful stories and beliefs, because they have nothing to lose and so do not fear, and the artists have made all the rest, because Providence has filled them with recklessness. All these look backward to a long tradition, for, being without fear, they have held to whatever pleased them. The others being always anxious have come to possess little that is good in itself, and are always changing from thing to thing, for whatever they do or have must be a means to something else, and they have so little belief that anything can be an end in itself, that they cannot understand you if you say 'All the most valuable things are useless.' They prefer the stalk to the flower, and believe that painting and poetry exist that there may be instruction, and love that there may be children, and theatres that busy men may rest, and holidays that busy men may go on being busy. At all times they fear and even hate the things that have worth in themselves, for that worth may suddenly, as it were a fire, consume their book of Life, where the world is represented by cyphers and symbols; and before all else, they fear irreverent joy and unserviceable sorrow. It seems to them, that those who have been freed by position, by poverty, or by the traditions of Art, have something terrible about them, a light that is unendurable to eyesight. They complain much of that commandment that we can do almost what we will, if we do it gaily, and think that freedom is but a trifling with the world.

If we would find a company of our own way of thinking, we must go backward to turreted walls, to courts, to high rocky places, to little walled towns, to jesters like that jester of Charles the Fifth who made mirth out of his own death; to the Duke Guidobaldo in his sickness, or Duke Frederick in his strength, to all those who understood that life is not lived at all, if not lived for contemplation or excitement.

Certainly we could not delight in that so courtly thing, the poetry of light love, if it were sad; for only when we are gay over a thing, and can play with it, do we show ourselves its master, and have minds clear enough for strength. The raging fire and the destructive sword are portions of eternity, too great for the eye of man, wrote Blake, and it is only before such things, before a love like that of Tristan and Iseult, before noble or ennobled death, that the free mind permits itself aught but brief sorrow. That we may be free from all the rest, sullen anger, solemn virtue, calculating anxiety, gloomy suspicion, prevaricating hope, we should be reborn in gaiety. Because there is submission in a pure sorrow, we should sorrow alone over what is greater than ourselves, nor too soon admit that greatness, but all that is less than we are should stir us to some joy, for pure joy masters and impregnates; and so to world end, strength shall laugh and wisdom mourn.

III

In life, courtesy and self-possession, and in the arts style, are the sensible impressions of the free mind, for both arise out of a deliberate shaping of all things, and from never being swept away, whatever the emotion, into confusion or dulness. The Japanese have numbered with heroic things courtesy at all times whatsoever, and though a writer, who has to withdraw so much of his thought out of his life that he may learn his craft, may find many his betters in daily courtesy, he should never be without style, which is but high breeding in words and in argument. He is indeed the Creator of the standards of manners in their subtlety, for he alone can know the ancient records and be like some mystic courtier who has stolen the keys from the girdle of time, and can wander where it please him amid the splendours of ancient courts.

Sometimes, it may be, he is permitted the license of cap and bell, or even the madman's bunch of straws, but he never forgets or leaves at home the seal and the signature. He has at all times the freedom of the well-bred, and being bred to the tact of words can take what theme he pleases, unlike the bourgeoisie, who are rightly compelled to be very strict in their conversation. Who should be free if he were not? for none other has a continual deliberate self-delighting happiness—style, 'the only thing that is immortal in literature,' as Sainte-Beuve has said, a still unexpended energy, after all that the argument or the story need, a still unbroken pleasure after the immediate end has been accomplished—and builds this up into a most personal and wilful fire, transfiguring words and sounds and events. It is the playing of strength when the day's work is done, a secret between a craftsman and his craft, and is so inseparate in his nature, that he has it most of all amid overwhelming emotion, and in the face of death. Shakespeare's persons when the last darkness has gathered about them, speak out of an ecstasy that is one half the self-surrender of sorrow, and one half the last playing and mockery of the victorious sword, before the defeated world.

It is in the arrangement of events as in the words, and in that touch of extravagance, of irony, of surprise, which is set there after the desire of logic has been satisfied and all that is merely necessary established, and that leaves one, not in the circling necessity, but caught up into the freedom of self-delight; as it were, the foam upon the cup, the long pheasant's feather on the horse's head, the spread peacock over the pasty. If it be very conscious, very deliberate, as it may be in comedy, for comedy is more personal than tragedy, we call it phantasy, perhaps even mischievous phantasy, recognising how disturbing it is to all that drag a ball at the ankle. This joy, because it must be always making and mastering, remains in the hands and in the tongue of the artist, but with his eyes he enters upon a submissive, sorrowful contemplation of the great irremediable things, and he is known from other men by making all he handles like himself, and yet by the unlikeness to himself of all that comes before him in a pure contemplation. It may have been his enemy or his love or his cause that set him dreaming, and certainly the phœnix can but open her young wings in a flaming nest; but all hate and hope vanishes in the dream, and if his mistress brag of the song or his enemy fear it, it is not that either has its praise or blame, but that the twigs of the holy nest are not easily set afire. The verses may make his mistress famous as Helen or give a victory to his cause, not because he has been either's servant, but because men delight to honour and to remember all that have served contemplation. It had been easier to fight, to die even, for Charles's house with Marvel's poem in the memory, but there is no zeal of service that had not been an impurity in the pure soil where the marvel grew. Timon of Athens contemplates his own end, and orders his tomb by the beachy margent of the flood, and Cleopatra sets the asp to her bosom, and their words move us because their sorrow is not their own at tomb or asp, but for all men's fate. That shaping joy has kept the sorrow pure, as it had kept it were the emotion love or hate, for the nobleness of the Arts is in the mingling of contraries, the extremity of sorrow, the extremity of joy, perfection of personality, the perfection of its surrender, overflowing turbulent energy, and marmorean stillness; and its red rose opens at the meeting of the two beams of the cross, and at the trysting-place of mortal and immortal, time and eternity. No new man has ever plucked that rose, or found that trysting-place, for he could but come to the understanding of himself, to the mastery of unlocking words after long frequenting of the great Masters, hardly without ancestral memory of the like. Even knowledge is not enough, for the 'recklessness' or negligence which Castiglione thought necessary in good manners is necessary in this likewise, and if a man has it not he will be gloomy, and had better to his marketing again.

IV

WHEN I saw John O'Leary first, every young Catholic man who had intellectual ambition fed his imagination with the poetry of Young Ireland; and the verses of even the least known of its poets were expounded with a devout ardour at Young Ireland Societies and the like, and their birthdays celebrated. The School of writers I belonged to, tried to found itself on much of the subject-matter of this poetry, and, what was almost more in our thoughts, to begin a more imaginative tradition in Irish literature, by a criticism at once remorseless and enthusiastic. It was our criticism, I think, that set Clarence Mangan at the head of the Young Ireland poets in the place of Davis, and put Sir Samuel Ferguson, who had died with but little fame as a poet, next in the succession. Our attacks, mine especially, on verse which owed its position to its moral or political worth, roused a resentment which even I find it hard to imagine to-day, and our verse was attacked in return, and not for anything peculiar to ourselves, but for all that it had in common with the accepted poetry of the world, and most of all for its lack of rhetoric, its refusal to preach a doctrine or to consider the seeming necessities of a cause. Now, after so many years, I can see how natural, how poetical even, an opposition was, that shows what large numbers could not call up certain high feelings without accustomed verses, or believe we had not wronged the feeling when we did but attack the verses. I have just read in a newspaper that Sir Charles Gavan Duffy recited before his death his favourite poem, one of the worst of the patriotic poems of Young Ireland, and it has brought all this to mind, for the opposition to our School claimed him as its leader. When I was at Siena, I noticed that the Byzantine style persisted in faces of Madonnas for several generations after it had given way to a more natural style, in the less loved faces of saints and martyrs. Passion had grown accustomed to those sloping and narrow eyes, which are almost Japanese, and to those gaunt cheeks, and would have thought it sacrilege to change. We would not, it is likely, have found listeners if John O'Leary, the irreproachable patriot, had not supported us. It was as clear to him that a writer must not write badly, or ignore the examples of the great masters in the fancied or real service of a cause, as it was that he must not lie for it or grow hysterical. I believed in those days that a new intellectual life would begin, like that of Young Ireland, but more profound and personal, and that could we but get a few plain principles accepted, new poets and writers of prose would make an immortal music. I think I was more blind than Johnson, though I judge this from his poems rather than anything I remember of his talk, for he never talked ideas, but, as was common with his generation in Oxford, facts and immediate impressions from life. With others this renunciation was but a pose, a superficial reaction from the disordered abundance of the middle century, but with him it was the radical life. He was in all a traditionalist, gathering out of the past phrases, moods, attitudes, and disliking ideas less for their uncertainty than because they made the mind itself changing and restless. He measured the Irish tradition by another greater than itself, and was quick to feel any falling asunder of the two, yet at many moments they seemed but one in his imagination. Ireland, all through his poem of that name, speaks to him with the voice of the great poets, and in 'Ireland Dead' she is still mother of perfect heroism, but there doubt comes too.

> Can it be they do repent
>
> That they went, thy chivalry,
>
> Those sad ways magnificent.

And in 'Ways of War,' dedicated to John O'Leary, he dismissed the belief in an heroic Ireland as but a dream.

> A dream! A dream! an ancient dream!
>
> Yet ere peace come to Innisfail,
>
> Some weapons on some field must gleam,
>
> Some burning glory fire the Gael.

That field may lie beneath the sun,

Fair for the treading of an host:

That field in realms of thought be won,

And armed hands do their uttermost:

Some way, to faithful Innisfail,

Shall come the majesty and awe

Of martial truth, that must prevail

To lay on all the eternal law.

I do not think either of us saw that, as belief in the possibility of armed insurrection withered, the old romantic nationalism would wither too, and that the young would become less ready to find pleasure in whatever they believed to be literature. Poetical tragedy, and indeed all the more intense forms of literature, had lost their hold on the general mass of men in other countries as life grew safe, and the sense of comedy which is the social bond in times of peace as tragic feeling is in times of war, had become the inspiration of popular art. I always knew this, but I believed that the memory of danger, and the reality of it seemed near enough sometimes, would last long enough to give Ireland her imaginative opportunity. I could not foresee that a new class, which had begun to rise into power under the shadow of Parnell, would change the nature of the Irish movement, which, needing no longer great sacrifices, nor bringing any great risk to individuals, could do without exceptional men, and those activities of the mind that are founded on the exceptional moment.[D] John O'Leary had spent much of his thought in an unavailing war with the agrarian party, believing it the root of change, but the fox that crept into the badger's hole did not come from there. Power passed to small shop-keepers, to clerks, to that very class who had seemed to John O'Leary so ready to bend to the power of others, to men who had risen above the traditions of the countryman, without learning those of cultivated life or even educating themselves, and who because of their poverty, their ignorance, their superstitious piety, are much subject to all kinds of fear. Immediate victory, immediate utility, became everything, and the conviction, which is in all who have run great risks for a cause's sake, in the O'Learys and Mazzinis as in all rich natures, that life is greater than the cause, withered, and we artists, who are the servants not of any cause but of mere naked life, and above all of that life in its nobler forms, where joy and sorrow are one, Artificers of the Great Moment, became as elsewhere in Europe protesting individual voices. Ireland's great moment had passed, and she had filled no roomy vessels with strong sweet wine, where we have filled our porcelain jars against the coming winter.

August, 1907.

[112]
[113]

MODERN IRISH POETRY

Included by kind permission of Messrs. Methuen & Co.

THE Irish Celt is sociable, as may be known from his proverb, 'It is better to be quarreling than to be lonely,' and the Irish poets of the nineteenth century have made songs abundantly when friends and rebels have been at hand to applaud. The Irish poets of the eighteenth century found both at a Limerick hostelry, above whose door was written a rhyming welcome in Gaelic to all passing poets, whether their pockets were full or empty. Its owner, himself a famous poet, entertained his fellows as long as his money lasted, and then took to minding the hens and chickens of an old peasant woman for a living, and ended his days in rags, but not, one imagines, without content. Among his friends and guests had been Red O'Sullivan, Gaelic O'Sullivan, blind O'Heffernan, and many another, and their songs had made the people, crushed by the disasters of the Boyne and Aughrim, remember their ancient greatness.

The bardic order, with its perfect artifice and imperfect art, had gone down in the wars of the seventeenth century, and poetry had found shelter amid the turf smoke of the cabins. The powers that history commemorates are but the coarse effects of influences delicate and vague as the beginning of twilight, and these influences were to be woven like a web about the hearts of men by farm-labourers, pedlars, potato-diggers, hedge-schoolmasters, and grinders at the quern, poor wastrels who put the troubles of their native land, or their own happy or unhappy loves, into songs of an extreme beauty. But in the midst of this beauty was a flitting incoherence, a fitful dying out of the sense, as though the passion had become too great for words, as must needs be when life is the master and not the slave of the singer.

English-speaking Ireland had meanwhile no poetic voice, for Goldsmith had chosen to celebrate English scenery and manners; and Swift was but an Irishman by what Mr. Balfour has called the visitation of God, and much against his will; and Congreve by education and early association; while Parnell, Denham, and Roscommon were poets but to their own time. Nor did the coming with the new century of the fame of Moore set the balance even, for his Irish melodies are too often artificial and mechanical in their style when separated from the music that gave them wings. Whatever he had of high poetry is in *The Light of Other Days* and in *At the Mid Hour of Night*, which express what Matthew Arnold has taught us to call 'the Celtic melancholy,' with so much of delicate beauty in the meaning and in the wavering or steady rhythm that one knows not where to find their like in literature. His more artificial and mechanical verse, because of the ancient music that makes it seem natural and vivid, and because it has remembered so many beloved names and events and places, has had the influence which might have belonged to these exquisite verses had he written none but these.

An honest style did not come into English-speaking Ireland until Callanan wrote three or four naive translations from the Gaelic. *Shule Aroon* and *Kathleen O'More* had indeed been written for a good while, but had no more influence than Moore's best verses. Now, however, the lead of Callanan was followed by a number of translators, and they in turn by the poets of Young Ireland, who mingled a little learned from the Gaelic ballad-writers with a great deal learned from Scott, Macaulay, and Campbell, and turned poetry once again into a principal means for spreading ideas of nationality and patriotism. They were full of earnestness, but never understand that, though a poet may govern his life by his enthusiasms, he must, when he sits down at his desk, but use them as the potter the clay. Their thoughts were a little insincere, because they lived in the half-illusions of their admirable ideals; and their rhythms not seldom mechanical, because their purpose was served when they had satisfied the dull ears of the common man. They had no time to listen to the voice of the insatiable artist, who stands erect, or lies asleep waiting until a breath arouses him, in the art of every craftsman. Life was their master, as it had been the master of the poets who gathered in the Limerick hostelry, though it conquered them not by unreasoned love for a woman, or for native land, but by reasoned enthusiasm, and practical energy. No man was more sincere, no man had a less mechanical mind than Thomas Davis, and yet he is often a little insincere and mechanical in his verse. When he sat down to write he had so great a desire to make the peasantry courageous and powerful that he half believed them already 'the finest peasantry upon the earth,' and wrote not a few such verses as—

'Lead him to fight for native land,

His is no courage cold and wary;

The troops live not that could withstand

The headlong charge of Tipperary'—

and to-day we are paying the reckoning with much bombast. His little book has many things of this kind, and yet we honour it for its public spirit, and recognize its powerful influence with gratitude. He was in the main an orator influencing men's acts, and not a poet shaping their emotions, and the bulk of his influence has been good. He was, indeed, a poet of much tenderness in the simple love-songs *The Marriage*, *A Plea for Love*, and *Mary Bhan Astór*, and, but for his ideal of a fisherman defying a foreign soldiery, would have been as good in *The Boatman of Kinsale;* and once or twice when he touched upon some historic sorrow he forgot his hopes for the future and his lessons for the present, and made moving verse.

His contemporary, Clarence Mangan, kept out of public life and its half-illusions by a passion for books, and for drink and opium, made an imaginative and powerful style. He translated from the German, and imitated Oriental poetry, but little that he did on any but Irish subjects has a lasting interest. He is usually classed with the Young Ireland poets, because he contributed to their periodicals and shared their political views; but his style was formed before their movement began, and he found it the more easy for this reason, perhaps, to give sincere expression to the mood which he had chosen, the only sincerity literature knows of; and with happiness and cultivation might have displaced Moore. But as it was, whenever he had no fine ancient song to inspire him, he fell into rhetoric which was only lifted out of commonplace by an arid intensity. In his *Irish National Hymn*, *Soul and Country*, and the like, we look into a mind full of parched sands where the sweet dews have never fallen. A miserable man may think well and express himself with great vehemence, but he cannot make beautiful things, for Aphrodite never rises from any but a tide of joy. Mangan knew nothing of the happiness of the outer man, and it was only when prolonging the tragic exultation of some dead bard that he knew the unearthly happiness which clouds the outer man with sorrow, and is the fountain of impassioned art. Like those who had gone before him, he was the slave of life, for he had nothing of the self-knowledge, the power of selection, the harmony of mind, which enables the poet to be its master, and to mould the world to a trumpet for his lips. But O'Hussey's Ode over his outcast chief must live for generations because of the passion that moves through its powerful images and its mournful, wayward, and fierce rhythms.

'Though he were even a wolf ranging the round green woods,

Though he were even a pleasant salmon in the unchainable sea,

Though he were a wild mountain eagle, he could scarce bear, he,

This sharp, sore sleet, these howling floods.'

Edward Walsh, a village schoolmaster, who hovered, like Mangan, on the edge of the Young Ireland movement, did many beautiful translations from the Gaelic; and Michael Doheny, while out 'on his keeping' in the mountains after the collapse at Ballingarry, made one of the most moving of ballads; but in the main the poets who gathered about Thomas Davis, and whose work has come down to us in *The Spirit of the Nation*, were of practical and political, not of literary, importance.

Meanwhile Samuel Ferguson, William Allingham, and Aubrey de Vere were working apart from politics; Ferguson selecting his subjects from the traditions of the bardic age, and Allingham from those of his native Ballyshannon, and Aubrey de Vere wavering between English, Irish, and Catholic tradition. They were wiser than Young Ireland in the choice of their models, for, while drawing not less from purely Irish sources, they turned to the great poets of the world, Aubrey de Vere owing something of his gravity to Wordsworth, Ferguson much of his simplicity to Homer, while Allingham had trained an ear, too delicate to catch the tune of but a single master, upon the lyric poetry of many lands. Allingham was the best artist, but Ferguson had the more ample imagination, the more epic aim. He had not the subtlety of feeling, the variety of cadence of a great lyric poet, but he has touched, here and there, an epic vastness and *naïveté*, as in the description in *Congal* of the mire-stiffened mantle of the giant spectre Mananan mac Lir striking against his calves with as loud a noise as the mainsail of a ship 'when with the coil of all its ropes it beat the sounding mast.' He is frequently dull, for he often lacked the 'minutely appropriate words' necessary to embody those fine changes of feeling which enthral the attention; but his sense of weight and size, of action and tumult, has set him apart and solitary, an epic figure in a lyric age.

Allingham, whose pleasant destiny has made him the poet of his native town, and put *The Winding Banks of Erne* into the mouths of the ballad- singers of Ballyshannon, is, on the other hand, a master of 'minutely appropriate words,' and can wring from the luxurious sadness of the lover, from the austere sadness of old age, the last golden drop of beauty; but amid action and tumult he can but fold his hands. He is the poet of the melancholy peasantry of the West, and, as years go on, and voluminous histories and copious romances drop under the horizon, will take his place among those minor immortals who have put their souls into little songs to humble the proud.

The poetry of Aubrey de Vere has less architecture than the poetry of Ferguson and Allingham, and more meditation. Indeed, his few but ever memorable successes are enchanted islands in gray seas of stately impersonal reverie and description, which drift by and leave no definite recollection. One needs, perhaps, to perfectly enjoy him, a Dominican habit, a cloister, and a breviary.

These three poets published much of their best work before and during the Fenian movement, which, like Young Ireland, had its poets, though but a small number. Charles Kickham, one of the 'triumvirate' that controlled it in Ireland; John Casey, a clerk in a flour-mill; and Ellen O'Leary, the sister of Mr. John O'Leary, were at times very excellent. Their verse lacks, curiously enough, the oratorical vehemence of Young Ireland, and is plaintive and idyllic. The agrarian movement that followed produced but little poetry, and of that little all is forgotten but a vehement poem by Fanny Parnell and a couple of songs by T. D. Sullivan, who is a good song-writer, though not, as the writer has read on an election placard, 'one of the greatest poets who ever moved the heart of man.' But while Nationalist verse has ceased to be a portion of the propaganda of a party, it has been written, and is being written, under the influence of the Nationalist newspapers and of Young Ireland societies and the like. With an exacting conscience, and better models than Thomas Moore and the Young Irelanders, such beautiful enthusiasm could not fail to make some beautiful verses. But, as things are, the rhythms are mechanical, and the metaphors conventional; and inspiration is too often worshipped as a Familiar who labours while you sleep, or forget, or do many worthy things which are not spiritual things.

For the most part, the Irishman of our times loves so deeply those arts which build up a gallant personality, rapid writing, ready talking, effective speaking to crowds, that he has no thought for the arts which consume the personality in solitude. He loves the mortal arts which have given him a lure to take the hearts of men, and shrinks from the immortal, which could but divide him from his fellows. And in this century, he who does not strive to be a perfect craftsman achieves nothing. The poor peasant of the eighteenth century could make fine ballads by abandoning himself to the joy or sorrow of the moment, as the reeds abandon themselves to the wind which sighs through them, because he had about him a world where all was old enough to be steeped in emotion. But we cannot take to ourselves, by merely thrusting out our hands, all we need of pomp and symbol, and if we have not the desire of artistic perfection for an ark, the deluge of incoherence, vulgarity, and triviality will pass over our heads. If we had no other symbols but the tumult of the sea, the rusted gold of the thatch, the redness of the quicken-berry, and had never known the rhetoric of the platform and of the newspaper, we could do without laborious selection and rejection; but, even then, though we might do much that would be delightful, that would inspire coming times, it would not have the manner of the greatest poetry.

Here and there, the Nationalist newspapers and the Young Ireland societies have trained a writer who, though busy with the old models, has some imaginative energy; while the more literary writers, the successors of Allingham and Ferguson and De Vere, are generally more anxious to influence and understand Irish thought than any of their predecessors who did not take the substance of their poetry from politics. They are distinguished too by their deliberate art, and by their preoccupation with spiritual passions and memories.

The poetry of Lionel Johnson and Mrs. Hinkson is Catholic and devout, but Lionel Johnson's is lofty and austere, and like De Vere's never long forgets the greatness of his Church and the interior life whose expression it is, while Mrs. Hinkson is happiest when she puts emotions, that have the innocence of childhood, into symbols and metaphors from the green world about her. She has no reverie nor speculation, but a devout tenderness like that of St. Francis for weak instinctive things, old gardeners, old fishermen, birds among the leaves, birds tossed upon the waters. Miss Hopper belongs to that school of writers which embodies passions, that are not the less spiritual because no Church has put them into prayers, in stories and symbols from old Celtic poetry and mythology. The poetry of 'A.E.', at its best, finds its symbols and its stories in the soul itself, and has a more disembodied ecstasy than any poetry of our time. He is the chief poet of the school of Irish mystics, in which there are many poets besides many who have heard the words, 'If ye know these things, happy are ye if ye do them,' and thought the labours that bring the mystic vision more important than the labours of any craft.

Mr. Herbert Trench and Mrs. Shorter and 'Moira O'Neill' are more interested in the picturesqueness of the world than in religion. Mr. Trench and Mrs. Shorter have put old Irish stories into vigorous modern rhyme, and have written, the one in her *Ceann Dubh Deelish* and the other in *Come, let us make Love deathless*, lyrics that should become a lasting part of Irish lyric poetry. 'Moira O'Neill' has written pretty lyrics of Antrim life; but one discovers that Mrs. Hinkson or Miss Hopper, although their work is probably less popular, comes nearer to the peasant passion, when one compares their work and hers with that Gaelic song translated so beautifully by Dr. Sigerson, where a ragged man of the roads, having lost all else, is yet thankful for 'the great love gift of sorrow,' or with many songs translated by Dr. Hyde in his *Love Songs of Connacht*, or by Lady Gregory in her *Poets and Dreamers*.

Except some few Catholic and mystical poets and Professor Dowden in one or two poems, no Irishman living in Ireland has sung excellently of any but a theme from Irish experience, Irish history, or Irish tradition. Trinity College, which desires to be English, has been the mother of many verse writers and of few poets; and this can only be because she has set herself against the national genius, and taught her children to imitate alien styles and choose out alien themes, for it is not possible to believe that the educated Irishman alone is prosaic and uninventive. Her few poets have been awakened by the influence of the farm-labourers, potato-diggers, pedlars, and hedge- schoolmasters of the eighteenth century, and their imitators in this, and not by a scholastic life, which, for reasons easy for all to understand and for many to forgive, has refused the ideals of Ireland, while those of England are but far- off murmurs. An enemy to all enthusiasms, because all enthusiasms seemed her enemies, she has taught her children to look neither to the world about them, nor into their own souls, where some dangerous fire might slumber.

To remember that in Ireland the professional and landed classes have been through the mould of Trinity College or of English universities, and are ignorant of the very names of the best Irish writers, is to know how strong a wind blows from the ancient legends of Ireland, how vigorous an impulse to create is in her heart to-day. Deserted by the classes from among whom has come the bulk of the world's intellect, she struggles on, gradually ridding herself of incoherence and triviality, and slowly building up a literature in English, which, whether important or unimportant, grows always more unlike others; nor does it seem as if she would long lack a living literature in Gaelic, for the movement for the preservation of Gaelic, which has been so much more successful than anybody foresaw, has already its poets. Dr. Hyde has written Gaelic poems which pass from mouth to mouth in the west of Ireland. The country people have themselves fitted them to ancient airs, and many that can neither read nor write sing them in Donegal and Connemara and Galway. I have, indeed, but little doubt that Ireland, communing with herself in Gaelic more and more, but speaking to foreign countries in English, will lead many that are sick with theories and with trivial emotion to some sweet well-waters of primeval poetry.

P.S.—This essay, written in 1895, though revised from time to time, sounds strangely to my ears to-day. I still admire much that I then admired, but if I rewrote it now I should take more pleasure in the temper of our writers and deal more sternly with their achievement. The magnanimous integrity of their politics, and their own gallant impetuous minds, needed no commendation among the young Irishmen for whom I wrote, and a very little dispraise of their verses seemed an attack upon the nation itself. Taylor, the orator, a man of genius and of great learning, never forgave me what I have said of Davis here and elsewhere, and it is easier for me to understand his anger in this year than thirteen years ago when the lofty thought of men like Taylor and O'Leary was the strength of Irish nationality. A new tradition is being built up on Gaelic poetry and romance and on the writings of the school I belong to, but the very strength of the new foundations, their lack of obvious generalization, their instinctive nature, the impossibility of ill-educated minds shaping the finer material, has for the moment marred the moral temper among those who are young enough to feel the change.

April, 1908.

LADY GREGORY'S *CUCHULAIN OF MUIRTHEMNE*

Mr. Bullen has just shown me the fifth volume of this
edition of my writings, and I discover that a note to the stories
of *Red Hanrahan* has been forgotten by the printer. That note
should have said that I owe thanks to Lady Gregory, who
helped me to rewrite the stories of *Red Hanrahan* in the
beautiful country speech of Kiltartan, and nearer to the
tradition of the people among whom he, or some likeness of
him, drifted and is remembered.—*April 14, 1908.*

I

I THINK this book is the best that has come out of Ireland in my time. Perhaps I
should say that it is the best book that has ever come out of Ireland; for the
stories which it tells are a chief part of Ireland's gift to the imagination of the
world—and it tells them perfectly for the first time. Translators from the Irish
have hitherto retold one story or the other from some one version, and not often
with any fine understanding of English, of those changes of rhythm, for
instance, that are changes of the sense. They have translated the best and fullest
manuscripts they knew, as accurately as they could, and that is all we have the
right to expect from the first translators of a difficult and old literature. But few
of the stories really begin to exist as great works of imagination until somebody
has taken the best out of many manuscripts. Sometimes, as in Lady Gregory's
version of *Deirdre*, a dozen manuscripts have to give their best before the beads
are ready for the necklace. It has been as necessary also to leave out as to add,
for generations of copyists, who had often but little sympathy with the stories
they copied, have mixed versions together in a clumsy fashion, often repeating
one incident several times, and every century has ornamented what was once
a simple story with its own often extravagant ornament. One does not perhaps
exaggerate when one says that no story has come down to us in the form it had
when the story-teller told it in the winter evenings. Lady Gregory has done her
work of compression and selection at once so firmly and so reverently that I
cannot believe that anybody, except now and then for a scientific purpose, will
need another text than this, or than the version[E] of it the Gaelic League has
begun to publish in Modern Irish. When she has added her translations from
other cycles, she will have given Ireland its *Mabinogion*, its *Morte D'Arthur*,
its *Nibelungenlied*. She has already put a great mass of stories, in which the
ancient heart of Ireland still lives, into a shape at once harmonious and
characteristic; and without writing more than a very few sentences of her
own to link together

incidents or thoughts taken from different manuscripts, without adding more indeed than the story-teller must often have added to amend the hesitation of a moment. Perhaps more than all, she has discovered a fitting dialect to tell them in. Some years ago I wrote some stories of mediæval Irish life, and as I wrote I was sometimes made wretched by the thought that I knew of no kind of English that befitted them as the language of Morris's prose stories—that lovely crooked language—befitted his journeys to woods and wells beyond the world. I knew of no language to write about Ireland in but our too smooth, too straight, too logical modern English; but now Lady Gregory has discovered a speech as beautiful as that of Morris, and a living speech into the bargain. As she lived among her people she grew to love the beautiful speech of those who think in Irish, and to understand that it is as true a dialect of English as the dialect that Burns wrote in. It is some hundreds of years old, and age gives a language authority. One finds in it the vocabulary of the translators of the Bible, joined to an idiom which makes it tender, compassionate, and complaisant, like the Irish language itself. It is certainly well suited to clothe a literature which never ceased to be folk-lore even when it was recited in the Courts of Kings.

II

Lady Gregory could with less trouble have made a book that would have better pleased the hasty reader. She could have plucked away details, smoothed out characteristics till she had left nothing but the bare stories; but a book of that kind would never have called up the past, or stirred the imagination of a painter or a poet, and would be as little thought of in a few years as if it had been a popular novel.

The abundance of what may seem at first irrelevant invention in a story like the death of Conaire, is essential if we are to recall a time when people were in love with a story, and gave themselves up to imagination as if to a lover. One may think there are too many lyrical outbursts, or too many enigmatical symbols here and there in some other story, but delight will always overtake one in the end. One comes to accept without reserve an art that is half epical, half lyrical, like that of the historical parts of the Bible, the art of a time when perhaps men passed more readily than they do now from one mood to another, and found it harder than we do to keep to the mood in which one tots up figures or banters a friend.

III

The Church when it was most powerful created an imaginative unity, for it taught learned and unlearned to climb, as it were, to the great moral realities through hierarchies of Cherubim and Seraphim, through clouds of Saints and Angels who had all their precise duties and privileges. The story-tellers of Ireland, perhaps of every primitive country, created a like unity, only it was to the great æsthetic realities that they taught people to climb. They created for learned and unlearned alike, a communion of heroes, a cloud of stalwart witnesses; but because they were as much excited as a monk over his prayers, they did not think sufficiently about the shape of the poem and the story. One has to get a little weary or a little distrustful of one's subject, perhaps, before one can lie awake thinking how one will make the most of it. They were more anxious to describe energetic characters, and to invent beautiful stories, than to express themselves with perfect dramatic logic or in perfectly-ordered words. They shared their characters and their stories, their very images, with one another, and handed them down from generation to generation; for nobody, even when he had added some new trait, or some new incident, thought of claiming for himself what so obviously lived its own merry or mournful life. The wood-carver who first put a sword into St. Michael's hand would have as soon claimed as his own a thought which was perhaps put into his mind by St. Michael himself. The Irish poets had also, it may be, what seemed a supernatural sanction, for a chief poet had to understand not only innumerable kinds of poetry, but how to keep himself for nine days in a trance. They certainly believed in the historical reality of even their wildest imaginations. And so soon as Christianity made their hearers desire a chronology that would run side by side with that of the Bible, they delighted in arranging their Kings and Queens, the shadows of forgotten mythologies, in long lines that ascended to Adam and his Garden. Those who listened to them must have felt as if the living were like rabbits digging their burrows under walls that had been built by Gods and Giants, or like swallows building their nests in the stone mouths of immense images, carved by nobody knows who. It is no wonder that one sometimes hears about men who saw in a vision ivy-leaves that were greater than shields, and blackbirds whose thighs were like the thighs of oxen. The fruit of all those stories, unless indeed the finest activities of the mind are but a pastime, is the quick intelligence, the abundant imagination, the courtly manners of the Irish country people.

IV

William Morris came to Dublin when I was a boy, and I had some talk with him about these old stories. He had intended to lecture upon them, but 'the ladies and gentlemen'—he put a communistic fervour of hatred into the phrase—knew nothing about them. He spoke of the Irish account of the battle of Clontarf and of the Norse account, and said, that one saw the Norse and

Irish tempers in the two accounts. The Norseman was interested in the way things are done, but the Irishman turned aside, evidently well pleased to be out of so dull a business, to describe beautiful supernatural events. He was thinking, I suppose, of the young man who came from Aoibhill of the Grey Rock, giving up immortal love and youth, that he might fight and die by Murrough's side. He said that the Norseman had the dramatic temper, and the Irishman had the lyrical. I think I should have said with Professor Ker, epical and romantic rather than dramatic and lyrical, but his words, which have so great an authority, mark the distinction very well, and not only between Irish and Norse, but between Irish and other un-Celtic literatures. The Irish story-teller could not interest himself with an unbroken interest in the way men like himself burned a house, or won wives no more wonderful than themselves. His mind constantly escaped out of daily circumstance, as a bough that has been held down by a weak hand suddenly straightens itself out. His imagination was always running to Tir-nan-og, to the Land of Promise, which is as near to the country-people of to-day as it was to Cuchulain and his companions. His belief in its nearness, cherished in its turn the lyrical temper, which is always athirst for an emotion, a beauty which cannot be found in its perfection upon earth, or only for a moment. His imagination, which had not been able to believe in Cuchulain's greatness, until it had brought the Great Queen, the red-eyebrowed goddess, to woo him upon the battlefield, could not be satisfied with a friendship less romantic and lyrical than that of Cuchulain and Ferdiad, who kissed one another after the day's fighting, or with a love less romantic and lyrical than that of Baile and Aillinn, who died at the report of one another's deaths, and married in Tir-nan-og. His art, too, is often at its greatest when it is most extravagant, for he only feels himself among solid things, among things with fixed laws and satisfying purposes, when he has reshaped the world according to his heart's desire. He understands as well as Blake that the ruins of time build mansions in eternity, and he never allows anything, that we can see and handle, to remain long unchanged. The characters must remain the same, but the strength of Fergus may change so greatly, that he, who a moment before was merely a strong man among many, becomes the master of Three Blows that would destroy an army, did they not cut off the heads of three little hills instead, and his sword, which a fool had been able to steal out of its sheath, has of a sudden the likeness of a rainbow. A wandering lyric moon must knead and kindle perpetually that moving world of cloaks made out of the fleeces of Mananan; of armed men who change themselves into sea-birds; of goddesses who become crows; of trees that bear fruit and flower at the same time. The great emotions of love, terror, and friendship must alone remain untroubled by the moon in that world, which is still the world of the Irish country-people, who do not open their eyes very wide at the most miraculous change, at the most sudden enchantment. Its events, and things, and people are wild, and are like unbroken horses, that are so much more beautiful than horses that have learned to run between shafts. One thinks of actual life, when one reads those Norse stories, which had shadows of their decadence, so necessary were the proportions of actual life to their efforts, when a dying man remembered his heroism enough to look down at his wound and say, 'Those broad spears are coming into fashion'; but the Irish stories make us understand why the Greeks called myths the activities of the dæmons. The great virtues, the great joys, the great privations come in the myths, and, as it were, take mankind between their naked arms, and without putting off their divinity. Poets have chosen their themes more often from stories that are all, or half, mythological, than from history or stories that give one the sensation of history, understanding, as I think, that the imagination which remembers the proportions of life is but a long wooing, and that it has to forget them before it becomes the torch and the marriage-bed.

V

One finds, as one expects, in the work of men who were not troubled about any probabilities or necessities but those of emotion itself, an immense variety of incident and character and of ways of expressing emotion. Cuchulain fights man after man during the quest of the Brown Bull, and not one of those fights is like another, and not one is lacking in emotion or strangeness; and when one thinks imagination can do no more, the story of the Two Bulls, emblematic of all contests, suddenly lifts romance into prophecy. The characters too have a distinctness we do not find among the people of the *Mabinogion*, perhaps not even among the people of the *Morte D'Arthur*. We know we will be long forgetting Cuchulain, whose life is vehement and full of pleasure, as though he always remembered that it was to be soon over; or the dreamy Fergus who betrays the sons of Usnach for a feast, without ceasing to be noble; or Conal who is fierce and friendly and trustworthy, but has not the sap of divinity that makes Cuchulain mysterious to men, and beloved of women. Women indeed, with their lamentations for lovers and husbands and sons, and for fallen rooftrees and lost wealth, give the stories their most beautiful sentences; and, after Cuchulain, one thinks most of certain great queens—of angry, amorous Maeve, with her long pale face; of Findabair, her daughter, who dies of shame and of pity; of Deirdre, who might be some mild modern housewife but for her prophetic wisdom. If one does not set Deirdre's lamentations among the greatest lyric poems of the world, I think one may be certain that the wine-press of the poets has been trodden for one in vain; and yet I think it may be proud Emer, Cuchulain's fitting wife, who will linger longest in the memory. What a pure flame burns in her always, whether she is the newly-married wife fighting for precedence, fierce as some beautiful bird, or the confident housewife, who would awaken her husband from his magic sleep with mocking words; or the great queen who would get him out of the tightening net of his doom, by sending him into the Valley of the Deaf, with Niamh, his mistress, because he will be more obedient to her; or the woman whom sorrow has set with Helen and Iseult and Brunnhilda, and Deirdre, to share their immortality in the rosary of the poets.

"'And oh! my love!' she said, "we were often in one another's company, and it was happy for us; for if the world had been searched from the rising of the sun to sunset, the like would never have been found in one place, of the Black Sainglain and the Grey of Macha, and Laeg the chariot-driver, and myself and Cuchulain."

'And after that Emer bade Conal to make a wide, very deep grave for Cuchulain; and she laid herself down beside her gentle comrade, and she put her mouth to his mouth, and she said: "Love of my life, my friend, my sweetheart, my one choice of the men of the earth, many is the woman, wed or unwed, envied me until to-day; and now I will not stay living after you."'

VI

To us Irish these personages should be very moving, very important, for they lived in the places where we ride and go marketing, and sometimes they have met one another on the hills that cast their shadows upon our doors at evening. If we will but tell these stories to our children the Land will begin again to be a Holy Land, as it was before men gave their hearts to Greece and Rome and Judea. When I was a child I had only to climb the hill behind the house to see long, blue, ragged hills flowing along the southern horizon. What beauty was lost to me, what depth of emotion is still perhaps lacking in me, because nobody told me, not even the merchant captains who knew everything, that Cruachan of the Enchantments lay behind those long, blue, ragged hills!

March, 1902.

LADY GREGORY'S
GODS AND FIGHTING MEN

[148]
[149]

I

A FEW months ago I was on the bare Hill of Allen, 'wide Almhuin of Leinster,' where Finn and the Fianna are said to have had their house, although there are no earthen mounds there like those that mark the sites of old houses on so many hills. A hot sun beat down upon flowering gorse and flowerless heather; and on every side except the east, where there were green trees and distant hills, one saw a level horizon and brown boglands with a few green places and here and there the glitter of water. One could imagine that had it been twilight and not early afternoon, and had there been vapours drifting and frothing where there were now but shadows of clouds, it would have set stirring in one, as few places even in Ireland can, a thought that is peculiar to Celtic romance, as I think, a thought of a mystery coming not as with Gothic nations out of the pressure of darkness, but out of great spaces and windy light. The hill of Teamhair, or Tara, as it is now called, with its green mounds and its partly-wooded sides, and its more gradual slope set among fat grazing lands, with great trees in the hedgerows, had brought before one imaginations, not of heroes who were in their youth for hundreds of years, or of women who came to them in the likeness of hunted fawns, but of kings that lived brief and politic lives, and of the five white roads that carried their armies to the lesser kingdoms of Ireland, or brought to the great fair that had given Teamhair its sovereignty all that sought justice or pleasure or had goods to barter.

II

It is certain that we must not confuse these kings, as did the mediæval chroniclers, with those half-divine kings of Almhuin. The chroniclers, perhaps because they loved tradition too well to cast out utterly much that they dreaded as Christians, and perhaps because popular imagination had begun the mixture, have mixed one with another ingeniously, making Finn the head of a kind of Militia under Cormac MacArt, who is supposed to have reigned at Teamhair in the second century, and making Grania, who travels to enchanted houses under the cloak of Aengus, god of Love, and keeps her

76

troubling beauty longer than did Helen hers, Cormac's daughter, and giving the stories of the Fianna, although the impossible has thrust its proud finger into them all, a curious air of precise history. It is only when we separate the stories from that mediæval pedantry, as in this book, that we recognise one of the oldest worlds that man has imagined, an older world certainly than we find in the stories of Cuchulain, who lived, according to the chroniclers, about the time of the birth of Christ. They are far better known, and we may be certain of the antiquity of incidents that are known in one form or another to every Gaelic-speaking countryman in Ireland or in the Highlands of Scotland. Sometimes a labourer digging near to a cromlech, or Bed of Diarmuid and Grania as it is called, will tell one a tradition that seems older and more barbaric than any description of their adventures or of themselves in written text or in story that has taken form in the mouths of professed story-tellers. Finn and the Fianna found welcome among the court poets later than did Cuchulain; and one finds memories of Danish invasions and standing armies mixed with the imaginations of hunters and solitary fighters among great woods. One never hears of Cuchulain delighting in the hunt or in woodland things; and one imagines that the story-teller would have thought it unworthy in so great a man, who lived a well-ordered, elaborate life, and had his chariot and his chariot-driver and his barley-fed horses to delight in. If he is in the woods before dawn one is not told that he cannot know the leaves of the hazel from the leaves of the oak; and when Emer laments him no wild creature comes into her thoughts but the cuckoo that cries over cultivated fields. His story must have come out of a time when the wild wood was giving way to pasture and tillage, and men had no longer a reason to consider every cry of the birds or change of the night. Finn, who was always in the woods, whose battles were but hours amid years of hunting, delighted in the 'cackling of ducks from the Lake of the Three Narrows; the scolding talk of the blackbird of Doire an Cairn; the bellowing of the ox from the Valley of the Berries; the whistle of the eagle from the Valley of Victories or from the rough branches of the Ridge of the Stream; the grouse of the heather of Cruachan; the call of the otter of Druim re Coir.' When sorrow comes upon the queens of the stories, they have sympathy for the wild birds and beasts that are like themselves: 'Credhe wife of Cael came with the others and went looking through the bodies for her comely comrade, and crying as she went. And as she was searching she saw a crane of the meadows and her two nestlings, and the cunning beast the fox watching the nestlings; and when the crane covered one of the birds to save it, he would make a rush at the other bird, the way she had to stretch herself out over the birds; and she would sooner have got her own death by the fox than the nestlings to be killed by him. And Credhe was looking at that, and she said: "It is no wonder I to have such love for my comely sweetheart, and the bird in that distress about her nestlings."'

III

One often hears of a horse that shivers with terror, or of a dog that howls at something a man's eyes cannot see, and men who live primitive lives where instinct does the work of reason are fully conscious of many things that we cannot perceive at all. As life becomes more orderly, more deliberate, the supernatural world sinks farther away. Although the gods come to Cuchulain, and although he is the son of one of the greatest of them, their country and his are far apart, and they come to him as god to mortal; but Finn is their equal. He is continually in their houses; he meets with Bodb Dearg, and Aengus, and Mananan, now as friend with friend, now as with an enemy he overcomes in battle; and when he has need of their help his messenger can say: 'There is not a king's son or a prince, or a leader of the Fianna of Ireland, without having a wife or a mother or a foster-mother or a sweetheart of the Tuatha de Danaan.' When the Fianna are broken up at last, after hundreds of years of hunting, it is doubtful that he dies at all, and certain that he comes again in some other shape, and Oisin, his son, is made king over a divine country. The birds and beasts that cross his path in the woods have been fighting-men or great enchanters or fair women, and in a moment can take some beautiful or terrible shape. We think of him and of his people as great-bodied men with large movements, that seem, as it were, flowing out of some deep below the shallow stream of personal impulse, men that have broad brows and quiet eyes full of confidence in a good luck that proves every day afresh that they are a portion of the strength of things. They are hardly so much individual men as portions of universal nature, like the clouds that shape themselves and reshape themselves momentarily, or like a bird between two boughs, or like the gods that have given the apples and the nuts; and yet this but brings them the nearer to us, for we can remake them in our image when we will, and the woods are the more beautiful for the thought. Do we not always fancy hunters to be something like this, and is not that why we think them poetical when we meet them of a sudden, as in these lines in *Pauline*?——

'An old hunter
Talking with gods; or a high-crested chief
Sailing with troops of friends to Tenedos.'

IV

One must not expect in these stories the epic lineaments, the many incidents, woven into one great event of, let us say, the story of the War for the Brown Bull of Cuailgne, or that of the last gathering at Muirthemne. Even *Diarmuid and Grania*, which is a long story, has nothing of the clear outlines of *Deirdre*, and is indeed but a succession of detached episodes. The men who imagined the Fianna had the imagination of children, and as soon as they had invented one wonder, heaped another on top of it. Children—or, at any rate, it is so I remember my own childhood—do not understand large design, and they delight in little shut-in places where they can play at houses more than in great expanses where a country-side takes, as it were, the impression of a thought. The wild creatures and the green things are more to them than to us, for they creep towards our light by little holes and crevices. When they imagine a country for themselves, it is always a country where one can wander without aim, and where one can never know from one place what another will be like, or know from the one day's adventure what may meet one with to-morrow's sun. I have wished to become a child again that I might find this book, that not only tells me of such a country, but is fuller than any other book that tells of heroic life, of the childhood that is in all folk-lore, dearer to me than all the books of the western world.

V

Children play at being great and wonderful people, at the ambitions they will put away for one reason or another before they grow into ordinary men and women. Mankind as a whole had a like dream once; everybody and nobody built up the dream bit by bit, and the ancient story-tellers are there to make us remember what mankind would have been like, had not fear and the failing will and the laws of nature tripped up its heels. The Fianna and their like are themselves so full of power, and they are set in a world so fluctuating and dream-like, that nothing can hold them from being all that the heart desires.

I have read in a fabulous book that Adam had but to imagine a bird and it was born into life, and that he created all things out of himself by nothing more important than an unflagging fancy; and heroes who can make a ship out of a shaving have but little less of the divine prerogatives. They have no speculative thoughts to wander through eternity and waste heroic blood; but how could that be otherwise? for it is at all times the proud angels who sit thinking upon the hill-side and not the people of Eden. One morning we meet them hunting a stag that is 'as joyful as the leaves of a tree in summer-time'; and whatever they do, whether they listen to the harp or follow an enchanter over-sea, they do for the sake of joy, their joy in one another, or their joy in pride and movement; and even their battles are fought more because of their delight in a good fighter than because of any gain that is in victory. They live always as if they were playing a game; and so far as they have any deliberate purpose at all, it is that they may become great gentlemen and be worthy of the songs of poets. It has been said, and I think the Japanese were the first to say it, that the four essential virtues are to be generous among the weak, and truthful among one's friends, and brave among one's enemies, and courteous at all times; and if we understand by courtesy not merely the gentleness the story-tellers have celebrated, but a delight in courtly things, in beautiful clothing and in beautiful verse, one understands that it was no formal succession of trials that bound the Fianna to one another. Only the Table Round, that is indeed, as it seems, a rivulet from the same well-head, is bound in a like fellowship, and there the four heroic virtues are troubled by the abstract virtues of the cloister. Every now and then some noble knight builds himself a cell upon the hill-side, or leaves kind women and joyful knights to seek the vision of the Grail in lonely adventures. But when Oisin or some kingly forerunner—Bran, son of Febal, or the like—rides or sails in an enchanted ship to some divine country, he but looks for a more delighted companionship, or to be in love with faces that will never fade. No thought of any life greater than that of love, and the companionship of those that have drawn their swords upon the darkness of the world, ever troubles their delight in one another as it troubles Iseult amid her love, or Arthur amid his battles. It is one of the ailments of our speculation that thought, when it is not the planning of something, or the doing of something or some memory of a plain circumstance separates us from one another because it makes us always more unlike, and because no thought passes through another's ear unchanged. Companionship can only be perfect when it is founded on things, for things are always the same under the hand, and at last one comes to hear with envy the voices of boys lighting a lantern to ensnare moths, or of the maids chattering in the kitchen about the fox that carried off a turkey before breakfast. This book is full of fellowship untroubled like theirs, and made noble by a courtesy that has gone perhaps out of the world. I do not know in literature better friends and lovers. When one of the Fianna finds Osgar dying the proud death of a young man, and asks is it well with him, he is answered, 'I am as you would have me be.' The very heroism of the Fianna is indeed but their pride and joy in one another, their good fellowship. Goll, old and savage, and letting himself die of hunger in a cave because he is angry and sorry, can speak lovely words to the wife whose help he refuses. 'It is best as it is,' he said, 'and I never took the advice of a woman east or west, and I never will take it. And oh, sweet-voiced queen,' he said, 'what ails you to be fretting after me? And remember now your silver and your gold, and your silks … and do not be crying tears after me, queen with the white hands,' he said, 'but remember your constant lover Aodh, son of the best woman of the world, that came from Spain asking for you, and that I fought on Corcar-an-Dearg; and go to him now,' he said, 'for it is bad when a woman is without a good man.'

VI

They have no asceticism, but they are more visionary than any ascetic, and their invisible life is but the life about them made more perfect and more lasting, and the invisible people are their own images in the water. Their gods may have been much besides this, for we know them from fragments of mythology picked out with trouble from a fantastic history running backward to Adam and Eve, and many things that may have seemed wicked to the monks who imagined that history, may have been altered or left out; but this they must have been essentially, for the old stories are confirmed by apparitions among the country-people to-day. The Men of Dea fought against the mis-shapen Fomor, as Finn fights against the Cat-Heads and the Dog- Heads; and when they are overcome at last by men, they make themselves houses in the hearts of hills that are like the houses of men. When they call men to their houses and to their Country Under-Wave they promise them all that they have upon earth, only in greater abundance. The god Midhir sings to Queen Etain in one of the most beautiful of the stories: 'The young never grow old; the fields and the flowers are as pleasant to be looking at as the blackbird's eggs; warm streams of mead and wine flow through that country; there is no care or no sorrow on any person; we see others, but we ourselves are not seen.' These gods are indeed more wise and beautiful than men; but men, when they are great men, are stronger than they are, for men are, as it were, the foaming tide-line of their sea. One remembers the Druid who answered, when some one asked him who made the world, 'The Druids made it.' All was indeed but one life flowing everywhere, and taking one quality here, another there. It sometimes seems to one as if there is a kind of day and night of religion, and that a period when the influences are those that shape the world is followed by a period when the greater power is in influences that would lure the soul out of the world, out of the body. When Oisin is speaking with St. Patrick of the friends and the life he has outlived, he can but cry out constantly against a religion that has no meaning for him. He laments, and the country-people have remembered his words for centuries: 'I will cry my fill, but not for God, but because Finn and the Fianna are not living.'

VII

Old writers had an admirable symbolism that attributed certain energies to the influence of the sun, and certain others to the lunar influence. To lunar influence belong all thoughts and emotions that were created by the community, by the common people, by nobody knows who, and to the sun all that came from the high disciplined or individual kingly mind. I myself imagine a marriage of the sun and moon in the arts I take most pleasure in; and now bride and bridegroom but exchange, as it were, full cups of gold and silver, and now they are one in a mystical embrace. From the moon come the folk-songs imagined by reapers and spinners out of the common impulse of their labour, and made not by putting words together, but by mixing verses and phrases, and the folk-tales made by the capricious mixing of incidents known to everybody in new ways, as one deals out cards, never getting the same hand twice over. When one hears some fine story, one never knows whether it has not been hazard that put the last touch of adventure. Such poetry, as it seems to me, desires an infinity of wonder or emotion, for where there is no individual mind there is no measurer-out, no marker-in of limits. The poor fisher has no possession of the world and no responsibility for it; and if he dreams of a love-gift better than the brown shawl that seems too common for poetry, why should he not dream of a glove made from the skin of a bird, or shoes made from the skin of a herring, or a coat made from the glittering garment of the salmon? Was it not Æschylus who said he but served up fragments from the banquet of Homer?—but Homer himself found the great banquet on an earthen floor and under a broken roof. We do not know who at the foundation of the world made the banquet for the first time, or who put the pack of cards into rough hands; but we do know that, unless those that have made many inventions are about to change the nature of poetry, we may have to go where Homer went if we are to sing a new song. Is it because all that is under the moon thirsts to escape out of bounds, to lose itself in some unbounded tidal stream, that the songs of the folk are mournful, and that the story of the Fianna, whenever the queens lament for their lovers, reminds us of songs that are still sung in country-places? Their grief, even when it is to be brief like Grania's, goes up into the waste places of the sky. But in supreme art or in supreme life there is the influence of the sun too, and the sun brings with it, as old writers tell us, not merely discipline but joy; for its discipline is not of the kind the multitudes impose upon us by their weight and pressure, but the expression of the individual soul turning itself into a pure fire and imposing its own pattern, its own music, upon the heaviness and the dumbness that is in others and in itself. When we have drunk the cold cup of the moon's intoxication, we thirst for something beyond ourselves, and the mind flows outward to a natural immensity; but if we have drunk from the hot cup of the sun, our own fulness awakens, we desire little, for wherever one goes one's heart goes too; and if any ask what music is the sweetest, we can but answer, as Finn answered, 'What happens.' And yet the songs and stories that have come from either influence are a part, neither less than the other, of the pleasure that is the bride-bed of poetry.

VIII

Gaelic-speaking Ireland, because its art has been made, not by the artist choosing his material from wherever he has a mind to, but by adding a little to something which it has taken generations to invent, has always had a popular literature. We cannot say how much that literature has done for the vigour of the race, for who can count the hands its praise of kings and high-hearted queens made hot upon the sword-hilt, or the amorous eyes it made lustful for strength and beauty? We remember indeed that when the farming people and the labourers of the towns made their last attempt to cast out England by force of arms they named themselves after the companions of Finn. Even when Gaelic has gone, and the poetry with it, something of the habit of mind remains in ways of speech and thought and 'come-all-ye's' and poetical saying; nor is it only among the poor that the old thought has been for strength or weakness. Surely these old stories, whether of Finn or Cuchulain, helped to sing the old Irish and the old Norman-Irish aristocracy to their end. They heard their hereditary poets and story-tellers, and they took to horse and died fighting against Elizabeth or against Cromwell; and when an English- speaking aristocracy had their place, it listened to no poetry indeed, but it felt about it in the popular mind an exacting and ancient tribunal, and began a play that had for spectators men and women that loved the high wasteful virtues. I do not think that their own mixed blood or the habit of their time need take all, or nearly all, credit or discredit for the impulse that made our gentlemen of the eighteenth century fight duels over pocket-handkerchiefs, and set out to play ball against the gates of Jerusalem for a wager, and scatter money before the public eye; and at last, after an epoch of such eloquence the world has hardly seen its like, lose their public spirit and their high heart and grow querulous and selfish as men do who have played life out not heartily but with noise and tumult. Had they known the people and the game a little better, they might have created an aristocracy in an age that has lost the understanding of the word. When one reads of the Fianna, or of Cuchulain, or of some great hero, one remembers that the fine life is always a part played finely before fine spectators. There also one notices the hot cup and the cold cup of intoxication; and when the fine spectators have ended, surely the fine players grow weary, and aristocratic life is ended. When O'Connell covered with a dark glove the hand that had killed a man in the duelling-field, he played his part; and when Alexander stayed his army marching to the conquest of the world that he might contemplate the beauty of a plane-tree, he played his part. When Osgar complained as he lay dying of the keening of the women and the old fighting-men, he too played his part; 'No man ever knew any heart in me,' he said, 'but a heart of twisted horn, and it covered with iron; but the howling of the dogs beside me,' he said, 'and the keening of the old fighting-men and the crying of the women one after another, those are the things that are vexing me.' If we would create a great community—and what other game is so worth the labour?—we must recreate the old foundations of life, not as they existed in that splendid misunderstanding of the eighteenth century, but as they must always exist when the finest minds and Ned the beggar and Seaghan the fool think about the same thing, although they may not think the same thought about it.

IX

When I asked the little boy who had shown me the pathway up the Hill of Allen if he knew stories of Finn and Oisin, he said he did not, but that he had often heard his grandfather telling them to his mother in Irish. He did not know Irish, but he was learning it at school, and all the little boys he knew were learning it. In a little while he will know enough stories of Finn and Oisin to tell them to his children some day. It is the owners of the land whose children might never have known what would give them so much happiness. But now they can read this book to those that shall come after them, and it will make Slieve-naman, Allen, and Benbulben, the great mountain that showed itself before me every day through all my childhood and was yet unpeopled, and half the country-sides of south and west, as populous with memories as are Dundealgan and Emain Macha and Muirthemne; and after a while somebody may take boy and girl to some famous place and say, 'This land where your fathers lived proudly and finely should be dear and dear and again dear'; and perhaps when many names have grown musical to their ears, a more imaginative love will have taught them a better service.

X

I need say nothing about the translation and arrangement of this book except that it is worthy to be put beside *Cuchulain of Muirthemne*. Such books should not be commended by written words but by spoken words, were that possible, for the written words commending a book, wherein something is done supremely well, remain, to sound in the ears of a later generation, like the foolish sound of church bells from the tower of a church when every pew is full.

Autumn, 1903.

[170]
[171]

MR. SYNGE AND HIS PLAYS

[172]
[173]

Six years ago I was staying in a students' hotel in the Latin quarter, and somebody, whose name I cannot recollect, introduced me to an Irishman, who, even poorer than myself, had taken a room at the top of the house. It was J. M. Synge, and I, who thought I knew the name of every Irishman who was working at literature, had never heard of him. He was a graduate of Trinity College, Dublin, too, and Trinity College does not, as a rule, produce artistic minds. He told me that he had been living in France and Germany, reading French and German Literature, and that he wished to become a writer. He had, however, nothing to show but one or two poems and impressionistic essays, full of that kind of morbidity that has its root in too much brooding over methods of expression, and ways of looking upon life, which come, not out of life, but out of literature, images reflected from mirror to mirror. He had wandered among people whose life is as picturesque as the middle ages, playing his fiddle to Italian sailors, and listening to stories in Bavarian woods, but life had cast no light into his writings. He had learned Irish years ago, but had begun to forget it, for the only language that interested him was that conventional language of modern poetry which has begun to make us all weary. I was very weary of it for I had finished *The Secret Rose*, and felt how it had separated my imagination from life, sending my Red Hanrahan, who should have trodden the same roads with myself, into some undiscoverable country. I said 'Give up Paris, you will never create anything by reading Racine, and Arthur Symons will always be a better critic of French literature. Go to the Arran Islands. Live there as if you were one of the people themselves; express a life that has never found expression.' I had just come from Arran, and my imagination was full of those gray islands where men must reap with knives because of the stones.

He went to Arran and became a part of its life, living upon salt fish and eggs, talking Irish for the most part, but listening also to the beautiful English which has grown up in Irish-speaking districts, and takes its vocabulary from the time of Malory and of the translators of the Bible, but its idiom and its vivid metaphor from Irish. When Mr. Synge began to write in this language, Lady Gregory had already used it finely in her translations of Dr. Hyde's lyrics and plays, or of old Irish literature, but she had listened with different ears. He made his own selection of word and phrase, choosing what would express his own personality. Above all, he made word and phrase dance to a very strange rhythm, which will always, till his plays have created their own tradition, be difficult to actors who have not learned it from his lips. It is essential, for it perfectly fits the drifting emotion, the dreaminess, the vague yet measureless desire, for which he would create a dramatic form. It blurs definition, clear edges, everything that comes from the will, it turns imagination from all that is of the present, like a gold background in a religious picture, and it strengthens in every emotion whatever comes to it from far off, from brooding memory and dangerous hope. When he brought *The Shadow of the Glen*, his first play, to the Irish National Theatre Society, the players were puzzled by the rhythm, but gradually they became certain that his woman of the glens, as melancholy as a curlew, driven to distraction by her own sensitiveness, her own fineness, could not speak with any other tongue, that all his people would change their life if the rhythm changed. Perhaps no Irish countryman had ever that exact rhythm in his voice, but certainly if Mr. Synge had been born a countryman, he would have spoken like that. It makes the people of his imagination a little disembodied; it gives them a kind of innocence even in their anger and their cursing. It is part of its maker's attitude towards the world, for while it makes the clash of wills among his persons indirect and dreamy, it helps him to see the subject-matter of his art with wise, clear-seeing, unreflecting eyes; to preserve the innocence of good art in an age of reasons and purposes. Whether he write of old beggars by the roadside, lamenting over the misery and ugliness of life, or of an old Arran woman mourning her drowned sons, or of a young wife married to an old husband, he has no wish to change anything, to reform anything; all these people pass by as before an open window, murmuring strange, exciting words.

If one has not fine construction, one has not drama, but if one has not beautiful or powerful and individual speech, one has not literature, or, at any rate, one has not great literature. Rabelais, Villon, Shakespeare, William Blake, would have known one another by their speech. Some of them knew how to construct a story, but all of them had abundant, resonant, beautiful, laughing, living speech. It is only the writers of our modern dramatic movement, our scientific dramatists, our naturalists of the stage, who have thought it possible to be like the greatest, and yet to cast aside even the poor persiflage of the comedians, and to write in the impersonal language that has come, not out of individual life, nor out of life at all, but out of necessities of commerce, of parliament, of board schools, of hurried journeys by rail.

If there are such things as decaying art and decaying institutions, their decay must begin when the element they receive into their care from the life of every man in the world, begins to rot. Literature decays when it no longer makes more beautiful, or more vivid, the language which unites it to all life; and when one finds the criticism of the student, and the purpose of the reformer, and the logic of the man of science, where there should have been the reveries of the common heart, ennobled into some raving Lear or unabashed Don Quixote. One must not forget that the death of language, the substitution of phrases as nearly impersonal as algebra for words and rhythms varying from man to man, is but a part of the tyranny of impersonal things. I have been reading through a bundle of German plays, and have found everywhere a desire not to express hopes and alarms common to every man that ever came into the world, but politics or social passion, a veiled or open propaganda. Now it is duelling that has need of reproof; now it is the ideas of an actress, returning from the free life of the stage, that must be contrasted with the prejudice of an old-fashioned town; now it is the hostility of Christianity and Paganism in our own day that is to find an obscure symbol in a bell thrown from its tower by spirits of the wood. I compare the work of these dramatists with the greater plays of their Scandinavian master, and remember that even he, who has made so many clear-drawn characters, has made us no abundant character, no man of genius in whom we could believe, and that in him also, even when it is Emperor and Galilean that are face to face, even the most momentous figures are subordinate to some tendency, to some movement, to some inanimate energy, or to some process of thought whose very logic has changed it into mechanism—always to something other than human life.

We must not measure a young talent, whether we praise or blame, with that of men who are among the greatest of our time, but we may say of any talent, following out a definition, that it takes up the tradition of great drama as it came from the hands of the masters who are acknowledged by all time, and turns away from a dramatic movement, which, though it has been served by fine talent, has been imposed upon us by science, by artificial life, by a passing order.

When the individual life no longer delights in its own energy, when the body is not made strong and beautiful by the activities of daily life, when men have no delight in decorating the body, one may be certain that one lives in a passing order, amid the inventions of a fading vitality. If Homer were alive to- day, he would only resist, after a deliberate struggle, the temptation to find his subject not in Helen's beauty, that every man has desired, nor in the wisdom and endurance of Odysseus that has been the desire of every woman that has come into the world, but in what somebody would describe, perhaps, as 'the inevitable contest,' arising out of economic causes, between the country-places and small towns on the one hand, and, upon the other, the great city of Troy, representing one knows not what 'tendency to centralization.'

Mr. Synge has in common with the great theatre of the world, with that of

Greece and that of India, with the creator of Falstaff, with Racine, a delight in language, a preoccupation with individual life. He resembles them also by a preoccupation with what is lasting and noble, that came to him, not as I think from books, but while he listened to old stories in the cottages, and contrasted what they remembered with reality. The only literature of the Irish country-people is their songs, full often of extravagant love, and their stories of kings and of kings' children. 'I will cry my fill, but not for God, but because Finn and the Fianna are not living,' says Oisin in the story. Every writer, even every small writer, who has belonged to the great tradition, has had his dream of an impossibly noble life, and the greater he is, the more does it seem to plunge him into some beautiful or bitter reverie. Some, and of these are all the earliest poets of the world, gave it direct expression; others mingle it so subtly with reality, that it is a day's work to disentangle it; others bring it near by showing one whatever is most its contrary. Mr. Synge, indeed, sets before us ugly, deformed or sinful people, but his people, moved by no practical ambition, are driven by a dream of that impossible life. That we may feel how intensely his woman of the glen dreams of days that shall be entirely alive, she that is 'a hard woman to please,' must spend her days between a sour- faced old husband, a man who goes mad upon the hills, a craven lad and a drunken tramp; and those two blind people of *The Well of the Saints* are so transformed by the dream, that they choose blindness rather than reality. He tells us of realities, but he knows that art has never taken more than its symbols from anything that the eye can see or the hand measure.

It is the preoccupation of his characters with their dream that gives his plays their drifting movement, their emotional subtlety. In most of the dramatic writing of our time, and this is one of the reasons why our dramatists do not find the need for a better speech, one finds a simple motive lifted, as it were, into the full light of the stage. The ordinary student of drama will not find anywhere in *The Well of the Saints* that excitement of the will in the presence of attainable advantages, which he is accustomed to think the natural stuff of drama, and if he see it played he will wonder why act is knitted to act so loosely, why it is all, as it were, flat, why there is so much leisure in the dialogue, even in the midst of passion. If he see the *Shadow of the Glen*, he will ask, why does this woman go out of her house? Is it because she cannot help herself, or is she content to go? Why is it not all made clearer? And yet, like everybody when caught up into great events, she does many things without being quite certain why she does them. She hardly understands at moments why her action has a certain form, more clearly than why her body is tall or short, fair or brown. She feels an emotion that she does not understand. She is driven by desires that need for their expression, not 'I admire this man,' or 'I must go, whether I will or no,' but words full of suggestion, rhythms of voice, movements that escape analysis. In addition to all this, she has something that she shares with none but the children of one man's imagination. She is intoxicated by a dream which is hardly understood by herself, but possesses her like something half-remembered on a sudden wakening.

While I write, we are rehearsing *The Well of the Saints*, and are painting for it decorative scenery, mountains in one or two flat colours and without detail, ash trees and red salleys with something of recurring pattern in their woven boughs. For though the people of the play use no phrase they could not use in daily life, we know that we are seeking to express what no eye has ever seen.

ABBEY THEATRE,
January 27, 1905.

LIONEL JOHNSON

[184]
[185]

CONTEMPORARY Irish poets believe in a spiritual life, invisible and troubling, and express this belief in their poetry. Contemporary English poets are interested in the glory of the world, like Mr. Rudyard Kipling; or in the order of the world, like Mr. William Watson; or in the passion of the world, like Mr. John Davidson; or in the pleasure of the world, like Mr. Arthur Symons. Mr. Francis Thompson, who has fallen under the shadow of Mr. Coventry Patmore, the poet of an older time and in protest against that time, is alone preoccupied with a spiritual life; and even he, except at rare moments, has less living fervour of belief than pleasure in the gleaming and scented and coloured symbols that are the footsteps where the belief of others has trodden. Ireland, upon the other hand, is creating in English a poetry as full of spiritual ardour as the poetry that praised in Gaelic *The Country of the Two Mists*, and *The Country of the Young*, and *The Country of the Living Heart*.

'A.E.' has written an ecstatic pantheistic poetry which reveals in all things a kind of scented flame consuming them from within. Miss Hopper, an unequal writer, whose best verses are delicate and distinguished, has no clear vision of spiritual things, but makes material things as frail and fragile as if they were but smouldering leaves, that we stirred in some mid-world of dreams, as 'the gossips' in her poem 'stir their lives' red ashes.' Mrs. Hinkson, uninteresting at her worst, as only uncritical and unspeculative writers are uninteresting, has sometimes expressed an impassioned and instinctive Catholicism in poems that are, as I believe, as perfect as they are beautiful, while Mr. Lionel Johnson has in his poetry completed the trinity of the spiritual virtues by adding Stoicism to Ecstasy and Asceticism. He has renounced the world and built up a twilight world instead, where all the colours are like the colours in the rainbow that is cast by the moon, and all the people as far from modern tumults as the people upon fading and dropping tapestries. He has so little interest in our pains and pleasures, and is so wrapped up in his own world, that one comes from his books wearied and exalted, as though one had posed for some noble action in a strange *tableau vivant* that cast its painful stillness upon the mind instead of the body. He might have cried with Axel, 'As for living, our servants will do that for us.' As Axel chose to die, he has chosen to live among his books and between two memories—the religious tradition of the Church of Rome and the political tradition of Ireland. From these he gazes upon the future, and whether he write of Sertorius or of Lucretius, or of Parnell or of 'Ireland's dead,' or of

'98, or of St. Columba or of Leo XIII., it is always with the same cold or scornful ecstasy. He has made a world full of altar lights and golden vestures, and murmured Latin and incense clouds, and autumn winds and dead leaves, where one wanders remembering martyrdoms and courtesies that the world has forgotten.

His ecstasy is the ecstasy of combat, not of submission to the Divine will; and even when he remembers that 'the old Saints prevail,' he sees the 'one ancient Priest' who alone offers the Sacrifice, and remembers the loneliness of the Saints. Had he not this ecstasy of combat, he would be the poet of those peaceful and unhappy souls, who, in the symbolism of a living Irish visionary, are compelled to inhabit when they die a shadowy island Paradise in the West, where the moon always shines, and a mist is always on the face of the moon, and a music of many sighs is always in the air, because they renounced the joy of the world without accepting the joy of God.

1899.

THE PATHWAY

[190]
[191]

Most of us who are writing books in Ireland to-day have some kind of a spiritual philosophy; and some among us when we look backward upon our lives see that the coming of a young Brahmin into Ireland helped to give our vague thoughts a shape. When we were schoolboys we used to discuss whatever we could find to read of mystical philosophy and to pass crystals over each others' hands and eyes and to fancy that we could feel a breath flowing from them as people did in a certain German book; and one day somebody told us he had met a Brahmin in London who knew more of these things than any book. With a courage which I still admire, we wrote and asked him to come and teach us, and he came with a little bag in his hand and *Marius the Epicurean* in his pocket, and stayed with one of us, who gave him a plate of rice and an apple every day at two o'clock; and for a week and all day long he unfolded what seemed to be all wisdom. He sat there beautiful, as only an Eastern is beautiful, making little gestures with his delicate hands, and to him alone among all the talkers I have heard, the delight of ordered words seemed nothing, and all thought a flight into the heart of truth.

We brought him, on the evening of his coming, to a certain club which still discusses everything with that leisure which is the compensation of unsuccessful countries; and there he overthrew or awed into silence whatever metaphysics the town had. And next day, when we would have complimented him, he was remorseful and melancholy, for was it not 'intellectual lust'? And sometimes he would go back over something he had said and explain to us that his argument had been a fallacy, and apologise as though he had offended against good manners. And once, when we questioned him of some event, he told us what he seemed to remember, but asked us not to give much weight to his memory, for he had found that he observed carelessly. He said, 'We Easterns are taught to state a principle carefully, but we are not taught to observe and to remember and to describe a fact. Our sense of what truthfulness is is quite different from yours.' His principles were a part of his being, while our facts, though he was too polite to say it, were doubtless a part of that bodily life, which is, as he believed, an error. He certainly did hold that we lived too much to understand the truth or to live long, for he remembered that his father, who had been the first of his family for two thousand years to leave his native village, had repeated over and over upon his deathbed, 'The West is dying because of its restlessness.' Once when he had spoken of some Englishman who had gone down the crater of Vesuvius, some listener adventured: 'We like men who do that kind of thing, because a man should not think too much of his life,' but was answered solidly, 'You do not think little of your lives, but you think so much of your lives that you would enjoy them everywhere, even in the crater of Vesuvius.' Somebody asked him if we should pray, but even prayer was too full of hope, of desire, of life, to have any part in that acquiescence that was his beginning of wisdom, and he answered that one should say, before sleeping: 'I have lived many lives. I have been a slave and a prince. Many a beloved has sat upon my knees, and I have sat upon the knees of many a beloved. Everything that has been shall be again.' Beautiful words, that I spoilt once by turning them into clumsy verse.

Nearly all that we call education was to him but a means to bring us under the despotism of life; and I remember the bewilderment of a schoolmaster who asked about the education of children and was told to 'teach them fairy tales, and that they did not possess even their own bodies.' I think he would not have taught anybody anything that had to be written in prose, for he said, very seriously, 'I have thought much about it, and I have never been able to discover any reason why prose should exist.' I think he would not have trained anybody in anything but in the arts and in philosophy, which sweeps the pathway before them, for he certainly thought, as William Blake did, that the 'imagination is the man himself,' and can, if it be strong enough, work every miracle. A man had come to him in London, and had said, 'My wife believes that you have the wisdom of the East and can cure her neuralgia, from which she has suffered for years.' He had answered: 'Are you certain that she believes that? because, if you are, I can cure her.' He had gone to her and made a circle round her and recited a poem in Sanscrit, and she had never had neuralgia since. He recited the poem to us, and was very disappointed because we did not know by the sound that it was a description of the spring. Not only did he think that the imaginative arts were the only things that were quite sinless, but he spent more than half a day proving, by many subtle and elaborate arguments, that 'art for art's sake' was the only sinless doctrine, for any other would hide the shadow of the world as it exists in the mind of God by shadows of the accidents and illusions of life, and was but Sadducean blasphemy. Religion existed also for its own sake; and every soul quivered between two emotions, the desire to possess things, to make them a portion of its egotism, and a delight in just and beautiful things for their own sake—and all religions were a doctrinal or symbolical crying aloud of this delight. He would not give his own belief a name for fear he might seem to admit that there could be religion that expressed another delight, and if one urged him too impetuously, he would look embarrassed and say, 'This body is a Brahmin.' All other parts of religion were unimportant, for even our desire of immortality was no better than our other desires. Before I understood him, I asked what he would answer to one who began the discussion by denying the immortality of the soul, for the accident of a discussion with religious people had set him grafting upon this stock, and he said, 'I would say to him, What has that to do with you?'

I remember these phrases and these little fragments of argument quite clearly, for their charm and their unexpectedness has made them cling to the memory; but when I try to remember his philosophy as a whole, I cannot part it from what I myself have built about it, or have gathered in the great ruined house of 'the prophetic books' of William Blake; but I am certain that he taught us by what seemed an invincible logic that those who die, in so far as they have imagined beauty or justice, are made a part of beauty or justice, and move through the minds of living men, as Shelley believed; and that mind overshadows mind even among the living, and by pathways that lie beyond the senses; and that he measured labour by this measure, and put the hermit above all other labourers, because, being the most silent and the most hidden, he lived nearer to the Eternal Powers, and showed their mastery of the world. Alcibiades fled from Socrates lest he might do nothing but listen to him all life long, and I am certain that we, seeking as youth will for some unknown deed and thought, all dreamed that but to listen to this man who threw the enchantment of power about silent and gentle things, and at last to think as he did, was the one thing worth doing and thinking; and that all action and all words that lead to action were a little vulgar, a little trivial. Ah, how many years it has taken me to awake out of that dream!

1900-1908.

A BIBLIOGRAPHY OF
THE WRITINGS
OF
WILLIAM BUTLER YEATS
BY
ALLAN WADE.

NOTE.

I began to make this bibliography a good many years ago, putting into an old note-book a list of all the writings of Mr. Yeats that I knew, and adding others from time to time, as chance led me to find them in newspapers or periodicals. I had no thought in doing this but my own pleasure, and it is with a kind of wonder that I see my notes taking the form of a book or part of a book at Mr. Bullen's beautiful Shakespeare Head Press.

I do not think the arrangement of the bibliography needs any explanation. I have not found it possible always to identify the first appearance of poems and essays, particularly in the earlier collections; nor have I thought it necessary to include a reference to every letter written by Mr. Yeats to the Press, since many of these have dealt merely with small points of fact in this or that controversy of the moment. But otherwise I have tried to make the work as complete as possible, and have given many details to serve as guides to those who would study the path along which beauty has come into the world. I have watched the roses blossoming in the garden, though I may not know the secret of their growth.

My thanks for help and suggestions are due to Mr. Yeats himself and to Mr. A. H. Bullen, Mrs. Tynan Hinkson, Miss A. E. F. Horniman, Mr. John Masefield and Mr. T. W. Rolleston. The details of the American editions of Mr. Yeats's books have been kindly supplied by Mr. John Quinn of New York.

ALLAN WADE.

June, 1908.

Accursed who brings to light of day
The writings I have cast away!
But blessed he that stirs them not
And lets the kind worm take the lot!

—W.B.Y.

PART I.—ORIGINAL WORKS.

1886.

Mosada. | A Dramatic Poem. | By | W. B. Yeats. | With a | Frontispiece Portrait of the Author | By J. B. Yeats. | Reprinted from the Dublin University Review. | Dublin: | Printed by Sealy, Bryers, and Walker, | 94, 95 and 96 Middle Abbey Street. | 1886.

The whole enclosed in decorated border.

8vo, pp. ii and 12. Light brown paper covers.

There is no title-page, the above description being taken from the front cover.

Mosada originally appeared in *The Dublin University Review*, June, 1886.

1889.

The Wanderings of Oisin | and other Poems | by | W. B. Yeats | London | Kegan Paul, Trench & Co., 1, Paternoster Square | 1889

Fcap. 8vo, pp. vi and 156. Cloth.

CONTENTS.

Originally appeared in *The Dublin University Review*, April, 1886.

A Legend.

An Old Song re-sung.

Street Dancers. This poem appeared in *The Leisure Hour*, March, 1890.

To an Isle in the Water.

Quatrains and Aphorisms. The first quatrain originally appeared in *The Dublin University Review*, February, 1886, under the title *Life*, and the second and sixth in January, 1886, under the title *In a Drawing Room*.

The Seeker. Originally appeared, under the title *The Seeker. A Dramatic Poem. In Two Scenes*, in *The Dublin University Review*, September, 1885.

Island of Statues. Originally appeared, under the title *The Island of Statues. An Arcadian Faery Tale. In Two Acts*, in *The Dublin University Review*, April, May, June and July, 1885.

1891.

Ganconagh | John Sherman | and | Dhoya | London | T. Fisher Unwin |
Paternoster Square | M DCCC XCI

24mo, pp. iv and 196. *The Pseudonym Library*, issued in yellow paper and in light brown linen. No.
10.

CONTENTS.

Ganconagh's Apology.

John Sherman.

Dhoya.

1892.

The | Countess Kathleen | and various Legends and Lyrics. | By | W. B. Yeats. | "He who tastes a crust of bread | tastes all the stars and all | the heavens." | Paracelsus ab Hohenheim | Cameo Series | T. Fisher Unwin Paternoster Sq. | London E.C. MDCCCXCII.

12mo, pp. 144. Paper boards with vellum back. Published in the Cameo Series. Frontispiece by J. T. Nettleship.

CONTENTS.

Preface.

The Countess Cathleen.

To the Rose upon the Rood of Time.

Fergus and the Druid. Originally appeared in *The National Observer*, May 21, 1891.

The Rose of the World. Originally appeared, under the title *Rosa Mundi*, in *The National Observer*, January 2, 1892.

The Peace of the Rose. Originally appeared in *The National Observer*, February 13, 1892.

The Death of Cuchullin. Originally appeared in *United Ireland*, June 11, 1892.

The White Birds. Originally appeared in *The National Observer*, May 7, 1892.

Father Gilligan. Originally appeared, under the title *Father Gilligan. (A Legend told by the People of Castleisland, Kerry.*), in *The Scots Observer*, July 5, 1890.

Father O'Hart. Appeared, under the title *The Priest of Coloony* in *Fairy and Folk Tales of the Irish Peasantry*, 1888.

When You are Old.

The Sorrow of Love.

The Ballad of the Old Foxhunter. Originally appeared in *East and West*, November, 1889.

A Fairy Song. Originally appeared in *The National Observer*, September 12, 1891.

The Pity of Love.

The Lake Isle of Innisfree. Originally appeared in *The National Observer*, December 13, 1890.

A Cradle Song. Originally appeared in *The Scots Observer*, April 19, 1890.

The Man who Dreamed of Fairy Land. Originally appeared, under the title *A Man who dreamed of Fairyland*, in *The National Observer*, February 7, 1891.

Dedication of Irish Tales. Originally appeared in *Representative Irish Tales*, 1890.

1893.

The Celtic Twilight. [in red] | Men and Women, Dhouls and | Faeries. | By | W. B. Yeats. | With a frontispiece by J. B. Yeats. | (Press mark of Lawrence and Bullen) | London: | Lawrence and Bullen, [in red] | 16, Henrietta St., Covent Garden. | 1893.

18mo, pp. xii and 212. Cloth.

CONTENTS.

Poem: *Time drops in decay*. Originally appeared, under the title *The Moods*, in *The Bookman*, Aug., 1893.

The Host. Originally appeared under the title *The Faery Host*, in *The National Observer*, October 7, 1893.

This Book.

A Teller of Tales. A part of this essay originally appeared in the introduction to *Fairy and Folk Tales of the Irish Peasantry*, 1888.

Belief and Unbelief. A part of this essay originally appeared in an essay *Irish Fairies* in *The Leisure Hour*, October, 1890.

A Visionary. Originally appeared, under the title *An Irish Visionary*, in *The National Observer*, October 3, 1891.

Village Ghosts. Originally appeared in *The Scots Observer*, May 11, 1889.

A Knight of the Sheep. Originally appeared, under the title *An Impression*, in *The Speaker*, October 21, 1893.

The Sorcerers.

The Last Gleeman. Originally appeared in *The National Observer*, May 6, 1893.

Regina, Regina Pigmeorum, Veni.

Kidnappers. Originally appeared in *The Scots Observer*, June 15, 1889.

The Untiring Ones.

The Man and his Boots.

A Coward.

The Three O'Byrnes and the Evil Faeries. Originally appeared as part of an essay *Irish Fairies* in *The Leisure Hour*, October, 1890.

Drumcliff and Rosses. Originally appeared, under the title *Columkille and Rosses*, in *The Scots Observer*, October 5, 1889.

The Thick Skull of the Fortunate.

The Religion of a Sailor.

Concerning the Nearness Together of Heaven, Earth and Purgatory.

The Eaters of Precious Stones.

Our Lady of the Hills. Originally appeared in *The Speaker*, November 11, 1893.

The Golden Age.

A Remonstrance with Scotsmen for having soured the disposition of their Ghosts and Faeries. Originally appeared under the title *Scots and Irish Fairies* in *The Scots Observer*, March 2, 1889.

The Four Winds of Desire.

Into the Twilight. Originally appeared, under the title *The Celtic Twilight* in *The National Observer*, July 29, 1893.

1894.

The Land | of Heart's | Desire | by | W. B. Yeats. | London: T. Fisher | Unwin, Paternoster | Square. MDCCCXCIV

The left-hand side of the title-page bears Aubrey Beardsley's design for the Avenue Theatre poster, much reduced in size and printed in black.

Sm. 4to, pp. 48. Pink paper cover, bearing reprint of the title-page.

1895.

Poems | By W. B. Yeats | London: Published by T. Fisher Unwin. | No. XI:
Paternoster Buildings: MDCCCXCV [The whole forms part of a design by H.G.F.]

Cr. 8vo, pp. xii and 288. Cloth.

CONTENTS.

Preface. (Dated Sligo, March 24, 1895.)

To Some I have talked with by the fire. Originally appeared in *The Bookman*,
May, 1895.

The Wanderings of Usheen.[F]

The Countess Cathleen.[G]

The Land of Heart's Desire.

The Rose:

> *To the Rose upon the Rood of Time.*[G]
>
> *Fergus and the Druid.*[G]
>
> *The Death of Cuhoolin.*[G]
>
> *The Rose of the World.*[G]
>
> *The Rose of Peace.*[G]
>
> *The Rose of Battle.*[G]
>
> *A Faery Song.*[G]
>
> *The Lake Isle of Innisfree.*[G]
>
> *A Cradle Song.*[G]
>
> *The Pity of Love.*[G]
>
> *The Sorrow of Love.*[G]
>
> *When You are Old.*[G]
>
> *The White Birds.*[G]
>
> *A Dream of Death.*[G]
>
> *A Dream of a Blessed Spirit.* Originally appeared, under
> the title *Kathleen*, in *The National Observer*,
> October 31, 1891.
>
> *The Man who Dreamed of Faeryland.*[G]
>
> *The Dedication to a Book of Stories selected from the
> Irish Novelists.*[G]
>
> *The Lamentation of the Old Pensioner.*[G]
>
> *The Ballad of Father Gilligan.*[G]
>
> *The Two Trees.*[G]
>
> *To Ireland in the Coming Times.*[G]

Crossways:

The Song of the Happy Shepherd.[F]

The Sad Shepherd.[F]

The Cloak, the Boat, and the Shoes.[F] (A re-writing of
the first lines of *Island of Statues.*)

Anashuya and Vijaya.[F]

The Indian upon God.[F]

The Indian to his Love.[F]

The Falling of the Leaves.[F]

Ephemera.[F]

The Madness of King Goll.[F]

The Stolen Child.[F]

To an Isle in the Water.[F]

Down by the Salley Gardens.[F]

The Meditation of the Old Fisherman.[F]

The Ballad of Father O'Hart.[G]

The Ballad of Moll Magee.[F]

The Ballad of the Foxhunter.[G]

Glossary.

1899. Second Edition, revised.

This edition has a portrait of the author by J. B. Yeats facing title-page, the preface is re-written, and the contents re-arranged thus:—

Preface. (Dated February 24, 1899.)

To Some I have talked with by the fire.

The Countess Cathleen.

The Rose.

The Land of Heart's Desire.

Crossways.

The Wanderings of Oisin.

Glossary.

1901. Third Edition, revised.

This edition has a new preface, dated January, 1901, and the note in the glossary on *The Countess Cathleen* is much enlarged.

1897.

The Secret Rose: [in red] | By W. B. Yeats, with | Illustrations by J. B. | Yeats. | (Press mark of Lawrence and Bullen) | Lawrence & Bullen, Limited, [in red] | 16 Henrietta Street, Covent Garden, | London, MDCCCXCVII.

Cr. 8vo, pp. xii and 268. Cloth.

CONTENTS.

Dedication to 'A.E.'

To the Secret Rose. Originally appeared, under the title *O'Sullivan Rua to the Secret Rose*, in *The Savoy*, September, 1896.

The Binding of the Hair. Originally appeared in *The Savoy*, January, 1896.

The Wisdom of the King. Originally appeared, under the title *Wisdom*, in *The New Review*, Sept., 1895.

Where there is Nothing, there is God. Originally appeared in *The Sketch*, October 21, 1896.

The Crucifixion of the Outcast. Originally appeared, under the title *A Crucifixion*, in *The National Observer*, March 24, 1894.

Out of the Rose. Originally appeared in *The National Observer*, May 27, 1893.

The Curse of the Fires and of the Shadows. Originally appeared in *The National Observer*, Aug. 5, 1893.

The Heart of the Spring. Originally appeared in *The National Observer*, April 15, 1893.

Of Costello the Proud, of Oona the Daughter of Dermott and of the Bitter Tongue. Originally appeared, under the title *Costello the Proud, Oona MacDermott and the Bitter Tongue*, in *The Pageant*, 1896.

The Book of the Great Dhoul and Hanrahan the Red. Originally appeared, under the title *The Devil's Book*, in *The National Observer*, November 26, 1892.

The Twisting of the Rope and Hanrahan the Red. Originally appeared, under the title *The Twisting of the Rope*, in *The National Observer*, December 24, 1892.

Kathleen the Daughter of Hoolihan and Hanrahan the Red. Originally appeared, under the title *Kathleen-ny-Houlihan*, in *The National Observer*, Aug. 4, 1894.

The Curse of Hanrahan the Red. Originally appeared, under the title *The Curse of O'Sullivan the Red upon Old Age*, in *The National Observer*, September 29, 1894.

The Vision of Hanrahan the Red. Originally appeared, under the title *The Vision of O'Sullivan the Red*, in *The New Review*, April, 1896.

The Death of Hanrahan the Red. Originally appeared, under the title *The Death of O'Sullivan the Red*, in *The New Review*, December, 1896.

The Rose of Shadow. Originally appeared under the title *Those Who Live in the Storm*, in *The Speaker*, July 21, 1894.

The Old Men of the Twilight. Originally appeared, under the title *St. Patrick and the Pedants*, in *The Weekly Sun Literary Supplement*, December 1, 1895.

Rosa Alchemica. Originally appeared in *The Savoy*, April, 1896.

The Tables of the Law. | The Adoration of the Magi. | By W. B. Yeats. | (Press mark of Lawrence and Bullen) | Privately Printed | MDCCCXCVII.

Cr. 8vo, pp. 48. Cloth. Portrait by J. B. Yeats facing title-page.

CONTENTS.

The Tables of the Law. Originally appeared in *The Savoy*, November, 1896.

The Adoration of the Magi.

One hundred and ten copies printed.

1904. First published edition:—

The Tables of the Law | and | The Adoration of the Magi | by | W. B. Yeats | London | Elkin Mathews, Vigo Street | 1904

Royal 16mo, pp. 60 and iv of advertisements. Paper covers. No. 17 of *The Vigo Cabinet Series.*

CONTENTS.

Prefatory Note.

The Tables of the Law.

The Adoration of the Magi.

Also an Edition de Luxe, limited.

1899.

The Wind | Among the Reeds | By | W. B. Yeats | London: Elkin Mathews | Vigo Street, W., 1899.

Cr. 8vo, pp. viii and 108. Cloth.

CONTENTS.

The Hosting of the Sidhe. For original appearance see under title *The Host*, in *The Celtic Twilight*, 1893.

The Everlasting Voices. Originally appeared, under the title *Everlasting Voices*, in *The New Review*, January, 1896.

The Moods. For original appearance see *The Celtic Twilight*, 1893.

Aedh tells of the Rose in his Heart. Originally appeared, under the title *The Rose in my Heart*, in *The National Observer*, November 12, 1892.

The Host of the Air. Originally appeared, under the title *The Stolen Bride*, in *The Bookman*, Nov., 1893.

Breasal the Fisherman. Originally appeared, under the title *Bressel the Fisherman*, in *The Cornish Magazine*, December, 1898.

A Cradle Song. Originally appeared as the first of *Two Poems concerning Peasant Visionaries*, in *The Savoy*, April, 1896.

Into the Twilight. For original appearance see *The Celtic Twilight*, 1893.

The Song of Wandering Aengus.

The Song of the Old Mother. Originally appeared in *The Bookman*, April, 1894.

The Fiddler of Dooney. Originally appeared in *The Bookman*, December, 1892.

The Heart of the Woman. Originally appeared in the story *The Rose of Shadow*, in *The Secret Rose*.

Aedh Laments the Loss of Love. Originally appeared as the second of *Aodh to Dectora. Three Songs*, in *The Dome*, May, 1898.

Mongan Laments the Change that has come upon him and his Beloved. Originally appeared, under the title *The Desire of Man and of Woman*, in *The Dome*, June, 1897.

Michael Robartes bids his Beloved be at Peace. Originally appeared, under the title *The Shadowy Horses*, in *The Savoy*, January, 1896.

Hanrahan reproves the Curlew. Originally appeared, under the title *Windlestraws. 1. O'Sullivan Rua to the Curlew*, in *The Savoy*, November, 1896.

Michael Robartes remembers forgotten Beauty. Originally appeared, under the title *O'Sullivan Rua to Mary Lavell*, in *The Savoy*, July, 1896.

A Poet to his Beloved. Originally appeared, under the title *O'Sullivan the Red to Mary Lavell*, in *The Senate*, March, 1896.

Aedh gives his Beloved certain Rhymes. Originally appeared in the story *The Binding of the Hair*. See *The Secret Rose*, 1897.

To my Heart, bidding it have no Fear. Originally appeared, under the title *Windlestraws*. 11. *Out of the Old Days*, in *The Savoy*, November, 1896.

The Cap and Bells. Originally appeared, under the title *Cap and Bell*, in *The National Observer*, March 17, 1894.

The Valley of the Black Pig. Originally appeared, as the second of *Two Poems concerning Peasant Visionaries*, in *The Savoy*, April, 1896.

Michael Robartes asks Forgiveness because of his many Moods. Originally appeared, under the title *The Twilight of Forgiveness*, in *The Saturday Review*, November 2, 1895.

Aedh tells of a Valley full of Lovers. Originally appeared under the title *The Valley of Lovers*, in *The Saturday Review*, January 9, 1897.

Aedh tells of the perfect Beauty. Originally appeared, under the title *O'Sullivan the Red to Mary Lavell*, in *The Senate*, March, 1896.

Aedh hears the Cry of the Sedge. Originally appeared as the first of *Aodh to Dectora. Three Songs*, in *The Dome*, May, 1898.

Aedh thinks of those who have spoken Evil of his Beloved. Originally appeared as the third of *Aodh to Dectora. Three Songs*, in *The Dome*, May, 1898.

The Blessed. Originally appeared in *The Yellow Book*, Volume XIII, April, 1897.

The Secret Rose. For original appearance see under *The Secret Rose*, 1897.

Hanrahan laments because of his Wanderings. Originally appeared, under the title *O'Sullivan the Red upon his Wanderings*, in *The New Review*, August, 1897.

The Travail of Passion. Originally appeared in *The Savoy*, January, 1896.

The Poet pleads with his Friend for old Friends. Originally appeared, under the title *Song*, in *The Saturday Review*, July 24, 1897.

Hanrahan Speaks to the Lovers of his Songs in coming Days. Originally appeared in the story *The Vision of Hanrahan the Red*. See *The Secret Rose*, 1897.

Aedh pleads with the Elemental Powers. Originally appeared, under the title *Aodh Pleads with the Elemental Powers*, in *The Dome*, December, 1898.

Aedh wishes his Beloved were dead.

Aedh wishes for the Cloths of Heaven.

Mongan thinks of his past Greatness. Originally appeared, under the title *Song of Mongan*, in *The Dome*, October, 1898.

Notes.

1900.

The Shadowy Waters | By W. B. Yeats | London: Hodder and | Stoughton |
27 Paternoster Row: MCM

Cr. 4to, pp. 60. Cloth.

CONTENTS.

I walked among the seven woods of Coole. Originally appeared, under the
title *Introduction to a Dramatic Poem*, in *The Speaker*, December 1,
1900.

The Shadowy Waters. Originally appeared in *The North American Review*,
May, 1900.

1902.

The Celtic Twilight [in red] | By W. B. Yeats | A. H. Bullen, [in red] 18 Cecil Court | St. Martin's Lane, London, W.C. | MCMII

Cr. 8vo, pp. x and 236. Cloth.

Portrait by J. B. Yeats facing title-page.

CONTENTS.

Poem: *Time drops in decay.*

The Hosting of the Sidhe.

This Book. I. 1893. II. 1902.

A Teller of Tales.

Belief and Unbelief.

Mortal Help. Originally appeared in The Speaker, April 19, 1902.

A Visionary. (With a new footnote.)

Village Ghosts.

'*Dust hath closed Helen's Eye.*' I. 1900. II. 1902. Part I originally appeared in *The Dome*, October, 1899.

A Knight of the Sheep.

An Enduring Heart. Originally appeared in *The Speaker*, April 26, 1902.

The Sorcerers. (With a new footnote.)

The Devil. Originally appeared in *The Speaker*, April 19, 1902.

Happy and Unhappy Theologians. Originally appeared in *The Speaker*, February 15, 1902.

The Last Gleeman.

Regina, Regina Pigmeorum Veni. (With a new footnote.)

'*And Fair, Fierce Women.*' Originally appeared in *The Speaker*, April 19, 1902.

Enchanted Woods. Originally appeared in *The Speaker*, January 18, 1902.

Miraculous Creatures. Originally appeared in *The Speaker*, April 26, 1902.

Aristotle of the Books. Originally appeared in *The Speaker*, April 19, 1902.

The Swine of the Gods. Originally appeared in *The Speaker*, April 19, 1902.

A Voice. Originally appeared in *The Speaker*, April 19, 1902.

Kidnappers. (With a new footnote.)

The Untiring Ones. (With a new footnote.)

Earth, Fire and Water. Originally appeared in *The Speaker*, March 15, 1902.

The Old Town. Originally appeared in *The Speaker*, March 15, 1902.

The Man and his Boots.

A Coward.

The Three O'Byrnes and the Evil Faeries.

Drumcliffe and Rosses.

The Thick Skull of the Fortunate. I. 1893. II. 1902.

The Religion of a Sailor.

Concerning the nearness together of Heaven, Earth and Purgatory. 1892 and 1902.

The Eaters of Precious Stones.

Our Lady of the Hills.

The Golden Age.

A Remonstrance with Scotsmen for having soured the disposition of their Ghosts and Faeries.

War. Originally appeared in *The Speaker*, March 15, 1902.

The Queen and the Fool. Originally appeared, under the title *The Fool of Faery*, in *The Kensington*, June, 1901.

The Friends of the People of Faery. Originally appeared as part of an essay, *The Tribes of Danu*, in *The New Review*, November, 1897.

Dreams that have no moral.

By the Roadside. Originally appeared in *An Claideamh Soluis*, July 13, 1901.

Into the Twilight.

Cathleen ni Hoolihan | A Play in One Act and | in Prose by W. B. Yeats | (ornament) [in red] | Printed at the Caradoc | Press Chiswick for A. H. | Bullen 18 Cecil Court Lon | don MDCCCCII

Pott 8vo, pp. vi (blank) and 34. Paper boards with leather back. Printed in red and black.

Cathleen ni Hoolihan originally appeared in *Samhain*, 1902.

1903.

Ideas of Good and [in red] | Evil. [in red] By W. B. Yeats | A. H. Bullen [in red] 47 Great Russell | Street, London, W.C. MCMIII

Cr. 8vo, pp. viii and 342. Paper boards with cloth back.

CONTENTS.

What is 'Popular Poetry?' Originally appeared in *The Cornhill Magazine*, March, 1902.

Speaking to the Psaltery. Originally appeared in *The Monthly Review*, May, 1902.

Magic. Originally appeared in *The Monthly Review*, September, 1901.

The Happiest of the Poets. Originally appeared in *The Fortnightly Review*, March, 1903.

The Philosophy of Shelley's Poetry:

    I. *His Ruling Ideas.* Originally appeared in *The Dome*, July, 1900.

    II. *His Ruling Symbols.*

At Stratford-on-Avon. Originally appeared in *The Speaker*, May 11 and 18, 1901.

William Blake and the Imagination. Originally appeared under the title *William Blake*, in *The Academy*, June 19, 1897.

William Blake and his Illustrations to the Divine Comedy:

    I. *His Opinions upon Art.* Originally appeared in *The Savoy*, July, 1896.

    II. *His Opinions upon Dante.* Originally appeared in *The Savoy*, August, 1896.

    III. *The Illustrations of Dante.* Originally appeared in *The Savoy*, September, 1896.

Symbolism in Painting. Originally appeared as part of the introduction to *A Book of Images*, 1898.

The Symbolism of Poetry. Originally appeared in *The Dome*, April, 1900.

The Theatre. The first section of this essay originally appeared in *The Dome*, April, 1899. The second originally appeared as part of an essay, *The Irish Literary Theatre*, 1900, in *The Dome*, Jan., 1900.

The Celtic Element in Literature. The first section of this essay originally appeared in *Cosmopolis*, June, 1898.

The Autumn of the Body. For original appearance see *The Autumn of the Flesh* in *Literary Ideals in Ireland.*

The Moods. Originally appeared as part of one of a series of articles on *Irish National Literature*, in *The Bookman*, August, 1895.

The Body of the Father Christian Rosencrux. Originally appeared as part of one of a series of articles on *Irish National Literature*, in *The Bookman*, September, 1895.

The Return of Ulysses. Originally appeared, under the title *Mr. Robert Bridges*, in *The Bookman*, June, 1897.

Ireland and the Arts. Originally appeared in *The United Irishman*, August 31, 1901.

The Galway Plains. Originally appeared, under the title *Poets and Dreamers*, in *The New Liberal Review*, March, 1903.

Emotion of Multitude.

Where There is Nothing: | being Volume One of Plays | for an Irish Theatre: by | W. B. Yeats | London: A. H. Bullen, 47, Great | Russell Street, W.C. 1903.

Cr. 8vo, pp. xii and 132. Paper boards with cloth back.

CONTENTS.

Dedication of Volumes One and Two of Plays for an Irish Theatre.

Where There is Nothing. Originally appeared as a supplement to *The United Irishman*, Samhain, (Autumn) 1902.

In the Seven Woods: being poems | chiefly of the Irish Heroic Age | By William Butler Yeats | The Dun Emer Press | Dundrum | MCMIII

8vo, pp. viii [unnumbered, i-iv blank] and 68 [the last four blank]. Linen with paper label. The book printed in red and black.

CONTENTS.

In the Seven Woods.

The Old Age of Queen Maeve. Originally appeared in *The Fortnightly Review*, April, 1903.

Baile and Aillinn. Originally appeared in *The Monthly Review*, July, 1902.

The Arrow.

The Folly of Being Comforted. Originally appeared in *The Speaker*, January 11, 1902.

The Withering of the Boughs. Originally appeared, under the title *Echtge of Streams*, in *The Speaker*, August 25, 1900.

Adam's Curse. Originally appeared in *The Monthly Review*, December, 1902.

The Song of Red Hanrahan. Originally appeared, under the title *Cathleen, Daughter of Hoolihan*, in *A Broadsheet*, April, 1903.

The Old Men admiring themselves in the Water. Originally appeared in *The Pall Mall Magazine*, January, 1903.

Under the Moon. Originally appeared in *The Speaker*, June 15, 1901.

The Players ask for a Blessing on the Psalteries and themselves.

The Rider from the North. Originally appeared, under the title *The Happy Townland*, in *The Weekly Critical Review*, June, 1903.

On Baile's Strand, a Play.

Edition limited to 325 copies.

The Hour-Glass | a Morality | By | W. B. Yeats | London | Wm. Heinemann, 21 Bedford St., W.C. | 1903

Demy 8vo, pp. 16 [the last two blank].

The Hour-Glass originally appeared in *The North American Review*, September, 1903.

A few copies only of this edition were printed, for purposes of copyright.

1904.

The Hour-Glass, Cathleen | ni Hoolihan, The Pot of | Broth: Being Volume Two of | Plays for an Irish Theatre: | By W. B. Yeats | London: A. H. Bullen, 47, Great | Russell Street, W.C. 1904.

Cr. 8vo, pp. viii and 84. Paper boards with cloth back.

CONTENTS.

The Hour-Glass: A Morality. For original appearance see above, under date 1903.

Cathleen ni Hoolihan. For original appearance see above, under date 1902.

The Pot of Broth.

Note on the Music.

The King's Threshold: and | On Baile's Strand: Being | Volume Three of Plays | for an Irish Theatre: By | W. B. Yeats | London: A. H. Bullen, 47, Great | Russell Street, W.C. 1904.

Cr. 8vo, pp. viii and 120. Paper boards with cloth back.

CONTENTS.

Note.

A Prologue. Originally appeared in *The United Irishman*, September 9, 1903.

[The Prologue, which was accidentally dropped from later editions, ran thus:—

A PROLOGUE.[H]

An Old Man *with a red dressing-gown, red slippers and red night-cap, holding a brass candlestick with a guttering candle in it, comes on from side of stage and goes in front of the dull green curtain.*

Old Man. I've got to speak the prologue. [*He shuffles on a few steps.*] My nephew, who is one of the play actors, came to me, and I in my bed, and my prayers said, and the candle put out, and he told me there were so many characters in this new play, that all the company were in it, whether they had been long or short at the business, and that there wasn't one left to speak the prologue. Wait a bit, there's a draught here. [*He pulls the curtain closer together.*] That's better. And that's why I am here, and maybe I'm a fool for my pains.

And my nephew said, there are a good many plays to be played for you, some to-night and some on other nights through the winter, and the most of them are simple enough, and tell out their story to the end. But as to the big play you are to see to-night, my nephew taught me to say what the poet had taught him to say about it. [*Puts down candlestick and puts right finger on left thumb.*] First, he who told the story of Seanchan on King Guaire's threshold long ago in the old books told it wrongly, for he was a friend of the king, or maybe afraid of the king, and so he put the king in the right. But he that tells the story now, being a poet, has put the poet in the right.

And then [*touches other finger*] I am to say: Some think it would be a finer tale if Seanchan had died at the end of it, and the king had the guilt at his door, for that might have served the poet's cause better in the end. But that is not true, for if he that is in the story but a shadow and an image of poetry had not risen up from the death that threatened him, the ending would not have been true and joyful enough to be put into the voices of players and proclaimed in the mouths of trumpets, and poetry would have been badly served.

[*He takes up the candlestick again.*

And as to what happened Seanchan after, my nephew told me he didn't know, and the poet didn't know, and it's likely there's nobody that knows. But my nephew thinks he never sat down at the king's table again, after the way he had been treated, but that he went to some quiet green place in the hills with Fedelm, his sweetheart, where the poor people made much of him because he was wise, and where he made songs and poems, and it's likely enough he made some of the old songs and the old poems the poor people on the hillsides are saying and singing to- day.

[*A trumpet-blast.*

Well, it's time for me to be going. That trumpet means that the curtain is going to rise, and after a while the stage there will be filled up with great ladies and great gentlemen, and poets, and a king with a crown on him, and all of them as high up in themselves with the pride of their youth and their strength and their fine clothes as if there was no such thing in the world as cold in the shoulders, and speckled shins, and the pains in the bones and the stiffness in the joints that make an old man that has the whole load of the world on him ready for his bed.

[*He begins to shuffle away, and then stops.*

And it would be better for me, that nephew of mine to be thinking less of his play-acting, and to have remembered to boil down the knap-weed with a bit of threepenny sugar, for me to be wetting my throat with now and again through the night, and drinking a sup to ease the pains in my bones.

[*He goes out at side of stage.*]

The King's Threshold.

On Baile's Strand. Originally appeared in *In the Seven Woods,* 1903.

Stories of Red Hanrahan by | William Butler Yeats | The Dun Emer Press | Dundrum MCMIV

8vo, pp. viii [unnumbered, i-ii blank] and 64 [last seven blank]. Paper boards with linen back, paper labels on front and side. The book printed in red and black; woodcut under Table of Contents on p. viii.

CONTENTS.

Edition limited to 500 copies.

These stories are a re-telling in simpler language of some of the stories in *The Secret Rose.*

1906.

Poems, 1899-1905 [in red] | By W. B. Yeats | London: A. H. Bullen | Dublin: Maunsel & Co., | Ltd. | 1906.

Cr. 8vo, pp. xvi and 280. Cloth.

CONTENTS.

Preface. [Dated *In the Seven Woods*, 18 May, 1906.]

I walked among the seven woods of Coole.[I]

The Harp of Aengus.[I]

The Shadowy Waters. [A new version.]

On Baile's Strand. [A new version.] *The Song of the Women* (pp. 102-104) originally appeared, under the title *Against Witchcraft*, in *The Shanachie* [No. I., Spring, 1906].

In the Seven Woods:

> *In the Seven Woods.*[J]
>
> *The Old Age of Queen Maeve.*[J]
>
> *Baile and Aillinn.*[J]
>
> *The Arrow.*[J]
>
> *The Folly of being Comforted.*[J]
>
> *Old Memory.* Originally appeared in *Wayfarer's Love*, 1904.
>
> *Never Give all the Heart.* Originally appeared in *McClure's Magazine*, December, 1905.
>
> *The Withering of the Boughs.*[I]
>
> *Adam's Curse.*[I]
>
> *The Song of Red Hanrahan.*[I]
>
> *The Old Men admiring themselves in the Water.*[I]
>
> *Under the Moon.*[I]
>
> *The Players ask for a Blessing on the Psalteries and themselves.*[I]
>
> *The Happy Townland.*[I]
>
> *The Entrance of Deirdre.* Two verses of this poem originally appeared, under the title *Queen Edaine*, in *McClure's Magazine*, September, 1905, and the whole poem under the title *The Praise of Deirdre*, in *The Shanachie* [No. I., Spring, 1906].

The King's Threshold. [A new version.]

Notes.

1907.

The Shadowy Waters, | By W. B. Yeats. | Acting Version, | As first played at the Abbey Theatre, December 8th, 1906. | A. H. Bullen, | 47 Great Russell Street, London, W.C. | 1907.

Cr. 8vo, pp. 28. Green paper cover.

This is a slightly different version from that printed in *Poems*, 1899-1905.

Deirdre By W. B. Yeats | Being Volume Five of Plays | for an Irish Theatre | London: A. H. Bullen | Dublin: Maunsel & Co., Ltd. | 1907.

Cr. 8vo, pp. viii and 48. Paper boards with cloth back.

CONTENTS.

Deirdre. For original appearance of the song *Why is it, Queen Edain said*, see *The Entrance of Deirdre*, in *Poems*, 1899-1905.

Note.

Discoveries; A Volume of Essays | By William Butler Yeats. | (Woodcut) | Dun Emer Press | Dundrum | MCMVII

8vo, pp. xvi [unnumbered, i-xi blank] and 56 [the last eleven blank]. Paper boards with linen back. The book printed in red and black.

CONTENTS.

Prophet, Priest and King.

Personality and the Intellectual Essences.

The Musician and the Orator.

A Banjo Player.

The Looking-glass.

> These five chapters appeared, under the general title *My Thoughts and my Second Thoughts*, in *The Gentleman's Magazine*, September, 1906.

The Tree of Life.

The Praise of Old Wives' Tales.

The Play of Modern Manners.

Has the Drama of Contemporary Life a Root of its Own?

Why the Blind Man in Ancient Times was made a Poet.

> These five chapters appeared, under the general title *My Thoughts and my Second Thoughts*, in The Gentleman's Magazine, October, 1906.

Concerning Saints and Artists.

The Subject Matter of Drama.

The Two Kinds of Asceticism.

In the Serpent's Mouth.

The Black and the White Arrows.

His Mistress's Eyebrows.

The Tresses of the Hair.

> These seven chapters appeared, under the general title *My Thoughts and my Second Thoughts*, in *The Gentleman's Magazine,* November, 1906.

A Tower on the Apennine.

The Thinking of the Body.

Religious Belief necessary to symbolic Art.

The Holy Places.

> These four chapters appeared, under the general title *Discoveries*, in The *Shanachie*, Autumn, 1907.

Edition limited to 200 copies.

1908.

The Collected Works in Verse and Prose of William Butler Yeats. Imprinted at the Shakespeare Head Press, Stratford-on-Avon, MCMVIII.

Eight volumes. Demy 8vo. Quarter vellum back with grey linen sides. With portraits by John S. Sargent, R.A., Signor Mancini, Charles Shannon and J. B. Yeats.

VOLUME I.

CONTENTS.

The Wind Among the Reeds.

The Old Age of Queen Maeve.

Baile and Aillinn.

In the Seven Woods.

Ballads and Lyrics.

The Rose.

The Wanderings of Oisin.

Notes.

A few poems have been moved from *The Wind Among the Reeds* to *Ballads and Lyrics* and *The Rose*. Two poems are added to *In the Seven Woods*. These are:—

The Hollow Wood. Originally appeared in *The Twisting of the Rope* in *Stories of Red Hanrahan*, 1904.

O do not love too long. Originally appeared in *The Acorn*, October, 1905.

VOLUME II.

The King's Threshold.

On Baile's Strand.

Deirdre.

The Shadowy Waters.

Appendix I: Acting Version of 'The Shadowy Waters.'

Appendix II: A different version of Deirdre's entrance.

Appendix III: The Legendary and Mythological Foundation of the Plays.

Appendix IV: The Dates and Places of Performance of Plays.

VOLUME III.

The Countess Cathleen.

The Land of Heart's Desire.

The Unicorn from the Stars. By Lady Gregory and W. B. Yeats.

Appendix: The Countess Cathleen.

Notes.

Music by Florence Farr and others.

VOLUME IV.

The Hour-Glass.

Cathleen ni Houlihan.

The Golden Helmet.

The Irish Dramatic Movement. Under this title are printed the greater part of Mr. Yeats's contributions to *Samhain*, 1901-1906, and to *The Arrow*, 1906-1907, and two essays, *An Irish National Theatre* and *The Theatre, the Pulpit, and the Newspapers*, which originally appeared in *The United Irishman*, October 10 and 17, 1903.

Appendix I: 'The Hour-Glass.'

Appendix II: 'Cathleen ni Hoolihan.'

Appendix III: 'The Golden Helmet.'

Appendix IV: Dates and Places of the First Performance of New Plays produced by the National Theatre Society and its predecessors.

VOLUME V.

The Celtic Twilight.

Stories of Red Hanrahan.

VOLUME VI.

Ideas of Good and Evil.

VOLUME VII.

The Secret Rose.

[The *Red Hanrahan* stories are here omitted from *The Secret Rose* as the later versions of them appear in Volume V. Two other stories which appeared in the volume of 1897 are also omitted.]

Rosa Alchemica.

The Tables of the Law.

The Adoration of the Magi.

John Sherman. With a new Preface.

Dhoya.

VOLUME VIII.

Discoveries.

Edmund Spenser. Originally appeared as the introduction to *Poems of Spenser*, 1906.

Poetry and Tradition.

Modern Irish Poetry. Originally appeared as the introduction to *A Book of Irish Verse*, 1895.

Lady Gregory's Cuchulain of Muirthemne. Originally appeared as the preface to *Cuchulain of Muirthemne*, 1902.

Lady Gregory's Gods and Fighting Men. Originally appeared as the preface to *Gods and Fighting Men*, 1904.

Mr. Synge and his Plays. Originally appeared as the introduction to *The Well of the Saints*, 1905.

Lionel Johnson. For original appearance see *A Treasury of Irish Poetry*, 1900.

The Pathway. Originally appeared, under the title *The Way of Wisdom*, in *The Speaker*, April 14, 1900.

PART II.

BOOKS EDITED OR CONTRIBUTED TO BY W. B. YEATS.

1888.

Poems and Ballads | of | Young Ireland | 1888 | "We're one at heart if you be Ireland's friend, | Though leagues asunder our opinions tend; | There are but two great parties in the end."| Allingham. | Dublin | M. H. Gill and Son | O'Connell Street | 1888

Fcap. 8vo, pp. viii and 80. White buckram.

Mr. Yeats's contributions are:—

> *The Stolen Child*, pp. 12-14.
>
> *King Goll* (*Third Century*), pp. 43-46. Originally appeared in *The Leisure Hour*, September, 1887.
>
> *The Meditation of the Old Fisherman*, p. 59. Originally appeared in *The Irish Monthly*, October, 1886.
>
> *Love Song. From the Gaelic*, p. 80.

Fairy and Folk Tales | of the Irish Peasantry: | Edited and Selected by | W. B. Yeats. London: | Walter Scott, 24 Warwick Lane. | New York: Thomas Whittaker | Toronto: W. J. Gage and Co. | 1888

Sm. cr. 8vo, pp. xx and 326. Cloth. A volume of *The Camelot Series* (afterwards *The Scott Library*).

Mr. Yeats's contributions are:—

> *Introduction*, pp. ix-xviii.
>
> *The Trooping Fairies*, pp. 1-3.
>
> *Notes* on pp. 16, 33, 38.
>
> *Changelings*, p. 47.
>
> *The Stolen Child*, pp. 59-60. Reprinted from *Poems and Ballads of Young Ireland*, 1888.
>
> *The Merrow*, p. 61.
>
> *The Solitary Fairies*, pp. 80-81.
>
> *The Pooka*, p. 94.
>
> *The Banshee*, p. 108.
>
> *Ghosts*, pp. 128-129.
>
> *Witches, Fairy Doctors*, pp. 146-149.
>
> *Note* on p. 150.
>
> *Tir-na-n-Og*, p. 200.
>
> *Saints, Priests*, p. 214.
>
> *The Priest of Coloony*, pp. 220-221.
>
> *Giants*, p. 260.
>
> *Notes*, pp. 319-326.

1893. Illustrated Edition.

Irish | Fairy and Folk Tales | Selected and Edited | with introduction | by W. B. Yeats. | Twelve Illustrations by James Torrance. | London: Walter Scott, Ltd. | 24 Warwick Lane.

Cr. 8vo, pp. xx and 326. Cloth.

1889.

Stories from Carleton: | With an introduction | by W. B. Yeats. | London: Walter Scott, 24 Warwick Lane. | New York and Toronto: | W. J. Gage & Co.

Sm. cr. 8vo, pp. xx and 302. Cloth. A volume of *The Camelot Classics* (afterwards *The Scott Library*).

Mr. Yeats's Introduction includes pp. ix-xvii.

1890.

Representative | Irish Tales | Compiled, with an Introduction and Notes | by | W. B. Yeats | First [Second] Series | (Ornament) | New York and London | G. P. Putnam's Sons | The Knickerbocker Press [Entire title printed on a yellow ground and enclosed within a red line border.]

32mo. Vol. I., pp. vi and 340. Vol. II., pp. iv and 356. Decorated boards with cloth backs.

Mr. Yeats's contributions are:—

VOLUME I.

Dedication. "There was a green branch hung with many a bell." Pp. iii-iv.

Introduction, pp. 1-17.

Maria Edgeworth, pp. 19-24.

John and Michael Banim, pp. 141-150.

William Carleton, pp. 191-196.

VOLUME II.

Samuel Lover, pp. 1-3.

William Maginn, pp. 91-92.

T. Crofton Croker, pp. 129-130.

Gerald Griffin, pp. 161-164.

Charles Lever, pp. 205-209.

Charles Kickham, pp. 243-245.

Miss Rosa Mulholland, p. 281.

Note, p. 331.

1892.

Irish | Fairy Tales | edited | with an introduction | by | W. B. Yeats | author of 'The Wanderings of Oisin,' etc. | Illustrated by Jack B. Yeats | London | T. Fisher Unwin | 1892

Fcap. 8vo, pp. viii and 236. Cloth. A volume of *The Children's Library*.

Mr. Yeats's contributions are:—

Poem. '*Where my books go.*' (Dated London, Jan., 1892.) P. v.

Introduction. 'An Irish Story-teller.' (Dated Clondalkin, July, 1891.) Pp. 1-7.

Note on pp. 8-9.

Appendix. Classification of Irish Fairies. (Dated Co. Down, June, 1891.) Pp. 223-233.

Authorities of Irish Folklore, pp. 234-236.

The Book | of the | Rhymers' Club | (Press mark) | London | Elkin Mathews | At the Sign of the Bodley Head | in Vigo Street | 1892 | All rights reserved

Royal 16mo, pp. xvi and 94. Paper boards.

Mr. Yeats's contributions are:—

A Man who dreamed of Fairyland, pp. 7-9. Originally appeared in *The National Observer*, February 7, 1891.

Father Gilligan, pp. 38-40. Originally appeared in *The Scots Observer*, July 5, 1890.

Dedication of 'Irish Tales,' pp. 54-55. Originally appeared in *Representative Irish Tales*, 1890.

A Fairy Song, p. 71. Originally appeared in *The National Observer*, September 12, 1891.

The Lake Isle of Innisfree, p. 84. Originally appeared in *The National Observer*, Dec. 13, 1890.

An Epitaph, p. 88. Originally appeared in *The National Observer*, December 12, 1891.

The | Poets [in red] | and the | Poetry [in red] | of the | Century [in red] | Charles Kingsley | to | James Thomson | Edited by [in red] | Alfred H. Miles [in red] | Hutchinson & Co. | 25, Paternoster Square, London

Post 8vo, pp. xx and 652. Cloth.

Mr. Yeats contributes a note on William Allingham, pp. 209-212.

The | Poets [in red] | and the | Poetry [in red] | of the | Century [in red] | Joanna Baillie | to | Mathilde Blind | Edited by [in red] | Alfred H. Miles [in red] | Hutchinson & Co. 25, Paternoster Square, London

Post 8vo, pp. xvi and 640. Cloth.

Mr. Yeats contributes a note on Ellen O'Leary, pp. 449-452.

1893.

The Works | of | William Blake | Poetic, Symbolic, and Critical | Edited with Lithographs of the Illustrated | "Prophetic Books," and a Memoir | and Interpretation | by | Edwin John Ellis | Author of "Fate in Arcadia," &c. | and| William Butler Yeats | Author of "The Wanderings of Oisin," "The Countess Kathleen," &c. | "Bring me to the test | And I the matter will reword, which madness | Would gambol from" | Hamlet | In Three Vols. | Vol. I. [II. III.] | London | Bernard Quaritch, 15 Piccadilly | 1893 | [All Rights Reserved]

Three volumes. Royal 8vo. Cloth.

The Poems | of | William Blake [in red] | Edited by | W. B. Yeats. | (Press mark of Lawrence and Bullen)

London:	New York:
in] Lawrence and Bullen [red	in] Charles Scribner's Sons [red
16 Henrietta Street, W.C.	743 & 745 Broadway
1893.	1893.

18mo, pp. liv and 252. Cloth. A volume of *The Muses' Library*.

Mr. Yeats's contributions are:—

Introduction, pp. xv-liv.

Notes, pp. 235-251.

1894.

The Second Book | of | The Rhymers' Club | London: Elkin Mathews &
John Lane | New York: Dodd, Mead & Company | 1894 | All rights reserved

Royal 16mo, pp. xvi and 136. Cloth.

Mr. Yeats's contributions are:—

> *The Rose in my Heart*, p. 11. Originally appeared in *The National Observer*,
> November 12, 1892.

> *The Folk of the Air*, pp. 37-39. Originally appeared, under the title *The Stolen
> Bride*, in *The Bookman*, November, 1893.

> *The Fiddler of Dooney*, pp. 68-69. Originally appeared in *The Bookman*,
> December, 1892.

> *A Mystical Prayer to the Masters of the Elements—Finvarra, Feacra, and
> Caolte*, pp. 91-92. Originally appeared, under the title *A Mystical
> Prayer to the Masters of the Elements, Michael, Gabriel, and
> Raphael*, in *The Bookman*, October, 1892.

> *The Cap and Bells*, pp. 108-109. Originally appeared, under the title *Cap
> and Bell*, in *The National Observer*, March 17, 1894.

> *The Song of the Old Mother*, p. 126. Originally appeared in *The Bookman*,
> April, 1894.

1895.

A Book of | Irish Verse | Selected from modern writers | with an introduction | and notes | by W. B. Yeats | Methuen & Co | 36 Essex Street, W.C. | London | 1895.

Cr. 8vo, pp. xxviii and 260. Linen.

Mr. Yeats's contributions are:—

Introduction. (Dated August 5, 1894.) Pp. xi-xxvii.

Acknowledgment, p. xxviii.

Notes, pp. 250-257.

1900. Revised edition.

This contains a new Preface, dated August 15, 1899, and the introduction much revised and now entitled *Modern Irish Poetry*. The selection of poetry is also revised.

1898.

A Book of Images | Drawn by W. T. | Horton & Intro-|duced by W. B. Yeats| London at the Unicorn | Press VII Cecil Court St. | Martin's Lane
MDCCCXCVIII

Fcap. 4to, pp. 62. Cloth. Number II. of *The Unicorn Quartos*.

Mr. Yeats's Introduction includes pp. 7-16.

1899.

Literary | Ideals in | Ireland. | By John Eglinton; | W. B. Yeats | A. E.; | W. Larminie. | Published by T. Fisher Unwin, London. | And at the Daily Express Office, Dublin.

Long 8vo, pp. ii and 88. Paper covers.

Mr. Yeats's contributions are:—

> *A Note on National Drama*, pp. 17-20. Originally appeared, as part of an essay under the title *The Poems and Stories of Miss Nora Hopper*, in *The Dublin Daily Express*, September 24, 1898.

> *John Eglinton and Spiritual Art*, pp. 31-37. Originally appeared in *The Dublin Daily Express*, October 29, 1898.

> *The Autumn of the Flesh*, pp. 69-75. Originally appeared in *The Dublin Daily Express*, December 3, 1898.

1899.-1900.

Beltaine. An Occasional Publication. Edited by W. B. Yeats.

No. 1. May, 1899.

Mr. Yeats's contributions are:—

Plans and Methods, pp. 6-9. Some of these notes originally appeared as part of an essay *The Irish Literary Theatre*, in *The Dublin Daily Express*, January 14, 1899.

Two lyrics, reprinted from *The Countess Cathleen*.

The Theatre. Originally appeared in *The Dome*, April, 1899.

No. 2. February, 1900.

Mr. Yeats's contributions are:—

Plans and Methods, pp. 3-6.

'Maive' and certain Irish Beliefs, pp. 14-17.

Footnote on p. 21.

The Irish Literary Theatre, 1900, pp. 22-24. Originally appeared in *The Dome*, January, 1900.

No. 3. April, 1900.

This number contained only an essay by Mr. Yeats entitled *'The Last Feast of the Fianna,' 'Maive,' and 'The Bending of the Bough' in Dublin.*

These three numbers were afterwards issued in one volume, with the wrappers and advertisements bound in, by the Unicorn Press in 1900.

1900.

A Treasury | of | Irish Poetry | in the | English Tongue | edited by | Stopford A. Brooke | and | T. W. Rolleston | London | Smith, Elder, & Co., 15 Waterloo Place | 1900 | All rights reserved

Cr. 8vo, pp. xliv and 580. Cloth.

Mr. Yeats contributes notes on:—

> *Lionel Johnson*, pp. 465-467. Originally appeared, under the title *Mr. Lionel Johnson and certain Irish Poets*, in *The Dublin Daily Express*, Aug. 27, 1898.
>
> *Nora Hopper*, pp. 471-473. Originally appeared as part of an essay *The Poems and Stories of Miss Nora Hopper*, in *The Dublin Daily Express*, September 24, 1898.
>
> *Althea Gyles*, p. 475.
>
> *A.E.*, pp. 485-487. Originally appeared under the title *The Poetry of A.E.*, in *The Dublin Daily Express*, September 3, 1898.

The book also reprints the following poems:—

> *The Hosting of the Sidhe.*
>
> *Michael Robartes remembers Forgotten Beauty.*
>
> *The Rose of the World.*
>
> *The Lake Isle of Innisfree.*
>
> *When you are Old.*
>
> *A Dream of a Blessed Spirit.*
>
> *The Lamentation of the Old Pensioner.*
>
> *The Two Trees.*
>
> *The Island of Sleep.* (A passage from *The Wanderings of Oisin*.)

146

1901.

Ideals in | Ireland | Edited by Lady Gregory | Written by "A.E.," D. P. | Moran, George Moore, | Douglas Hyde, Standish | O'Grady, and W. B. Yeats | London: At the Unicorn | VII Cecil Court MDCCCCI

Cr. 8vo, pp. 108. Cloth.

Mr. Yeats's contributions are:—

> *The Literary Movement in Ireland*, pp. 87-102. Originally appeared in *The North American Review*, December, 1899.
>
> *A Postscript*, pp. 105-107.

Samhain Edited | for the Irish Literary Theatre | by W. B. Yeats. | Published in October 1901 by | Sealy Bryers & Walker and | by T. Fisher Unwin.

Fcap. 4to, pp. 40. Brown paper covers.

Mr. Yeats's contributions are:—

> *Windlestraws*, pp. 3-10.
>
> *Footnote* on p. 12.

1902.

Cuchulain of Muirthemne: | The Story of the Men of | The Red Branch of Ulster | Arranged and put into | English by Lady Gregory. | With a Preface by W. B. Yeats | London | John Murray, Albemarle Street | 1902.

Large Cr. 8vo, pp. xx and 364. Cloth.

Mr. Yeats's contributions are:—

> *Preface.* (Dated March, 1902.) Pp. vii-xvii.
>
> *Note on the Conversation of Cuchulain and Emer*, pp. 351-353.

Samhain: An occasional | review edited by W. B. Yeats. | Published in October 1902 by | Sealy Bryers & Walker and | by T. Fisher Unwin.

Fcap. 4to, pp. 32. Brown paper covers.

Mr. Yeats's contributions are:—

> *Notes*, pp. 3-10.
>
> *Cathleen ni Hoolihan*, pp. 24-31.

1903.

Samhain: An occasional | review edited by W. B. Yeats. | Published in September 1903 | by Sealy Bryers & Walker | and by T. Fisher Unwin.

Fcap. 4to, pp. 36. Brown paper covers.

Mr. Yeats's contributions are:—

> *Notes*, pp. 3-8.
>
> *The Reform of the Theatre*, pp. 9-12. Part of this essay originally appeared in *The United Irishman*, April 4, 1903.

1904.

Gods and Fighting Men: | The Story of the Tuatha de | Danaan and of the Fianna | of Ireland, arranged and | put into English by Lady | Gregory. With a preface | by W. B. Yeats | London | John Murray, Albemarle Street, W. | 1904

Large cr. 8vo, pp. xxviii and 480.

Mr. Yeats's Preface includes pp. ix-xxiv.

Wayfarer's Love | Contributions from Living Poets | edited by | The Duchess of Sutherland. | Cover design by Mr. Walter Crane. | "Let me take your hand for love and sing you a song, | said the other traveller—the journey is a hard journey, but | if we hold together in the morning and in the evening, | what matter if in the hours between there is sorrow." | Old Tale. | Westminster | Archibald Constable & Co., Ltd. | 1904

Mr. Yeats contributes *Old Memory*, p. 37.

Samhain: An occasional | review edited by W. B. Yeats. | Published in December 1904 | by Sealy Bryers & Walker | and by T. Fisher Unwin.

Fcap. 4to, pp. 56. Brown paper covers.

Mr. Yeats's contributions are:—

The Dramatic Movement, pp. 3-12.

First Principles, pp. 12-24.

The Play, the Player, and the Scene, pp. 24-33.

Footnote to 'An Opinion,' p. 55.

1905.

Samhain: An occasional | review edited by W. B. Yeats. | Published in November 1905 | by Maunsel & Co., Ltd., | and by A. H. Bullen.

Mr. Yeats contributes *Notes and Opinions*, pp. 3-14.

The Well of the Saints. | By J. M. Synge. With an intro- | duction by W. B. Yeats. Be- | ing Volume Four of Plays | for an Irish Theatre | London: A. H. Bullen, 47, Great | Russell Street, W.C. 1905.

Cr. 8vo, pp. xviii and 92. Paper boards with cloth back.

Mr. Yeats's Introduction, *Mr. Synge and his Plays*, dated Abbey Theatre, January 27, 1905, includes pp. v-xvii.

1906.

Poems | of | Spenser | Selected and with | an Introduction by | W. B. Yeats. | T. C. & E. C. Jack. | Edinburgh. [The whole forms part of a design by A. S. Hartrick.]

Sm. cr. 8vo, pp. xlviii and 292. Cloth.

Mr. Yeats's Introduction includes pp. xiii-xlvii.

Samhain: An occasional | review edited by W. B. Yeats. | Published in December 1906 | by Maunsel & Co., Ltd., | Dublin.

Fcap. 4to, pp. 40. Brown paper covers.

Mr. Yeats's contributions are:—

Notes, p. 3.

Literature and the Living Voice, pp. 4-14. Originally appeared in *The Contemporary Review*, October, 1906.

1906-7.

The Arrow. Edited by W. B. Yeats.

Mr. Yeats's contributions are:—

No. 1. October 20, 1906.

The Season's Work.

A Note on The Mineral Workers.

Notes.

No. 2. November 24, 1906.

Notes.

Deirdre. (A note.)

The Shadowy Waters. (A note.)

No. 3. February 23, 1907.

The Controversy over 'The Playboy.'

Passages reprinted from the 'Samhain' of 1905.

Opening Speech at the debate of February 4 at the Abbey Theatre.

No. 4. June 1, 1907.

Notes.

NOTE.

The selections for the following books issued by the Dun Emer Press, Dundrum, were made by Mr. Yeats, but the books contain no contributions by him:—

Twenty-one *Poems* by Lionel Johnson, 1904.

Some Essays and Passages by John Eglinton, 1905.

Sixteen *Poems* by William Allingham, 1905.

Twenty-one *Poems* by Katherine Tynan, 1907.

PART III.

CONTRIBUTIONS TO PERIODICALS.

[This part gives a chronological list of Mr. Yeats's contributions to periodicals, including those that afterwards have been gathered into books. It seemed better to risk a certain amount of repetition in noting the later history of the collected writings than to set folk astray with a misleading list of titles.]

1885.

The Island of Statues. An Arcadian Faery Tale. In Two Acts. 'The Dublin University Review,' April-July. Reprinted under the title *Island of Statues* in *The Wanderings of Oisin*, 1889.

Love and Death. 'The Dublin University Review,' May.

The Seeker. A Dramatic Poem. In Two Scenes. 'The Dublin University Review,' September. Reprinted, under the title *The Seeker* in *The Wanderings of Oisin*, 1889.

An Epilogue. To The Island of Statues and The Seeker. 'The Dublin University Review,' October. Reprinted under the title *Song of the Last Arcadian* in *The Wanderings of Oisin*, 1889. Also under the title *The Song of the Happy Shepherd* in *Poems*, 1895; and in the *Collected Works*, Vol. I.

1886.

In a Drawing Room. (Unsigned.) 'The Dublin University Review,' January. Reprinted, as the sixth and second of *Quatrains and Aphorisms* in *The Wanderings of Oisin*, 1889.

Life. 'The Dublin University Review,' February. Five quatrains of which the first is reprinted as the first of *Quatrains and Aphorisms* in *The Wanderings of Oisin*, 1889.

The Two Titans. A Political Poem. 'The Dublin University Review,' March.

On Mr. Nettleship's Picture at the Royal Hibernian Academy. 'The Dublin University Review,' April. Reprinted in *The Wanderings of Oisin*, 1889.

Mosada. 'The Dublin University Review,' June. Reprinted in pamphlet form, 1886. Also in *The Wanderings of Oisin*, 1889.

Remembrance. 'The Irish Monthly,' July.

Miserrimus. 'The Dublin University Review,' October. Reprinted in *The Wanderings of Oisin*, 1889. Also, under the title *The Sad Shepherd* in *Poems*, 1895; and in the *Collected Works*, Vol. I.

From the Book of Kauri the Indian—Section V. On the Nature of God. (Unsigned.) 'The Dublin University Review,' October. Reprinted, under the title *Kanva, the Indian, on God* in *The Wanderings of Oisin*, 1889. Also, under the title *The Indian upon God* in *Poems*, 1895; and in the *Collected Works*, Vol. I.

Meditation of an Old Fisherman. 'The Irish Monthly,' October. Reprinted in *Poems and Ballads of Young Ireland*, 1888. Also in *The Wanderings of Oisin*, 1889; *Poems*, 1895; and in the *Collected Works*, Vol. I.

The Poetry of Sir Samuel Ferguson. 'The Irish Fireside,' October 9.

The Poetry of Sir Samuel Ferguson. 'The Dublin University Review,' November.

The Poetry of R. D. Joyce. 'The Irish Fireside,' November 27 and December 4.

The Stolen Child. 'The Irish Monthly,' December. Reprinted in *Poems and Ballads of Young Ireland*, 1888. Also in *Fairy and Folk Tales of the Irish Peasantry*, 1888; *The Wanderings of Oisin*, 1889; *Poems*, 1895; and in the *Collected Works*, Vol. I.

An Indian Song. 'The Dublin University Review,' December. Reprinted in *The Wanderings of Oisin*, 1889. Also, under the title *The Indian to his Love* in *Poems*, 1895; and in the *Collected Works*, Vol. I.

1887.

A Dawn-Song. 'The Irish Fireside,' February 5.

The Fairy Pedant. 'The Irish Monthly,' March. Reprinted in *The Wanderings of Oisin*, 1889.

Clarence Mangan. 'The Irish Fireside,' March 12.

Miss Tynan's New Book. 'The Irish Fireside,' July 9.

King Goll. An Irish Legend. 'The Leisure Hour,' September. Reprinted in *Poems and Ballads of Young Ireland*, 1888. Also in *The Wanderings of Oisin*, 1889; *Poems*, 1895; and in the *Collected Works*, Vol. I.

She who Dwelt among the Sycamores. 'The Irish Monthly,' September. Reprinted in *The Wanderings of Oisin*, 1889.

The Fairy Doctor. 'The Irish Fireside,' September, 10. Reprinted in *The Wanderings of Oisin*, 1889.

1889.

Scots and Irish Fairies. 'The Scots Observer,' March 2. Reprinted, under the title, *A Remonstrance with Scotsmen for having Soured the disposition of their Ghosts and Faeries*, in *The Celtic Twilight*, 1893 and 1902; and in the *Collected Works*, Vol. V.

Village Ghosts. 'The Scots Observer,' May 11. Reprinted in *The Celtic Twilight*, 1893 and 1902; and in the *Collected Works*, Vol. V.

Kidnappers. 'The Scots Observer,' June 15. Reprinted in *The Celtic Twilight*, 1893 and 1902; and in the *Collected Works*, Vol. V.

Columkille and Rosses. 'The Scots Observer,' October 5. Reprinted, under the title *Drumcliff and Rosses* in *The Celtic Twilight*, 1893 and 1902; and in the *Collected Works*, Vol. V.

The Ballad of the Old Foxhunter. 'East and West,' November. Reprinted in *The Countess Cathleen*, 1892. Also in *Poems*, 1895; and in the *Collected Works*, Vol. I.

Popular Ballad Poetry of Ireland. 'The Leisure Hour,' November.

1890.

Bardic Ireland. 'The Scots Observer,' January 4.

Street Dancers. 'The Leisure Hour,' March. This poem appeared in *The Wanderings of Oisin*, 1889.

Tales from the Twilight. 'The Scots Observer,' March 1.

A Cradle Song. 'The Scots Observer,' April 19. Reprinted in *The Countess Cathleen*, 1892. Also in *Poems*, 1895; and in the *Collected Works*, Vol. I.

Father Gilligan. (*A Legend told by the People of Castleisland, Kerry.*) 'The Scots Observer,' July 5. Reprinted in *The Book of the Rhymers' Club*, 1892. Also in *The Countess Cathleen*, 1892; *Poems*, 1895; and in the *Collected Works*, Vol. I.

Irish Fairies. 'The Leisure Hour,' October. Reprinted in part, under the titles *Belief and Unbelief*, and *The Three O'Byrnes and the Evil Faeries*, in *The Celtic Twilight*, 1893 and 1902; and in the *Collected Works*, Vol. V.

Poetry and Science in Folk-Lore. (A letter.) 'The Academy,' October 11.

The Old Pensioner. 'The Scots Observer,' November 15. Reprinted in *The Countess Cathleen*, 1892. Also in *Poems*, 1895; and in the *Collected Works*, Vol. I.

The Lake Isle of Innisfree. 'The National Observer,' December 13. Reprinted in *The Book of the Rhymers' Club*, 1892. Also in *The Countess Cathleen*, 1892; *Poems*, 1895; and in the *Collected Works*, Vol. I.

1891.

In the Firelight. (A poem.) 'The Leisure Hour,' Feb.

A Man who dreamed of Fairyland. 'The National Observer,' February 7. Reprinted in *The Book of the Rhymers' Club*, 1892. Also in *The Countess Cathleen*, 1892; *Poems*, 1895; and in the *Collected Works*, Vol. I.

Irish Folk Tales. 'The National Observer,' Feb. 28.

Some recent books by Irish Writers. 'The Boston Pilot,' April 18.

Plays by an Irish Poet. (The work of Dr. John Todhunter.) 'United Ireland,' July 11.

Clarence Mangan's Love Affair. 'United Ireland,' August 22.

A Fairy Song. 'The National Observer,' September 12. Reprinted in *The Book of the Rhymers' Club*, 1892. Also in *The Countess Cathleen*, 1892; *Poems*, 1895; and in the *Collected Works*, Vol. I.

A Reckless Century. Irish Rakes and Duellists. 'United Ireland,' September 12.

A Ballad Singer. 'The Boston Pilot,' September 12.

Oscar's Wilde's Last Book. (Review of *Lord Arthur Savile's Crime.*) 'United Ireland,' September 26.

An Irish Visionary. 'The National Observer,' October 3. Reprinted, under the title *A Visionary*, in *The Celtic Twilight*, 1893 and 1902; and in the *Collected Works*, Vol. V.

The Young Ireland League. 'United Ireland,' Oct. 3.

Mourn—and then Onward. (A poem.) 'United Ireland,' October 10.

Kathleen. 'The National Observer,' October 31. Reprinted, under the title *A Dream of a Blessed Spirit* in *Poems*, 1895. Also in the *Collected Works*, Vol. I.

An Epitaph. 'The National Observer,' December 12. Reprinted in *The Book of the Rhymers' Club*, 1892; and in *The Countess Cathleen*, 1892. Also under the title *A Dream of Death* in *Poems*, 1895; and in the *Collected Works*, Vol. I.

A Poet we have neglected. (William Allingham.) 'United Ireland,' December 12.

1892.

Rosa Mundi. 'The National Observer,' January 2. Reprinted, under the title *The Rose of the World*, in *The Countess Cathleen*, 1892. Also in *Poems*, 1895; and in the *Collected Works*, Vol. I.

The New 'Speranza.' (Miss Maud Gonne.) 'United Ireland,' January 16.

Dr. Todhunter's Irish Poems. (Review of *The Banshee*.) 'United Ireland,' January 23.

Clovis Huges on Ireland. 'United Ireland,' Jan. 30.

The Peace of the Rose. 'The National Observer,' Feb. 13. Reprinted in *The Countess Cathleen*, 1892. Also, under the title *The Rose of Peace*, in *Poems*, 1895; and in the *Collected Works*, Vol. I.

The White Birds. 'The National Observer,' May 7. Reprinted in *The Countess Cathleen*, 1892. Also in *Poems*, 1895; and in the *Collected Works*, Vol. I.

Fergus and the Druid. 'The National Observer,' May 21. Reprinted in *The Countess Cathleen*, 1892. Also in *Poems*, 1895; and in the *Collected Works*, Vol. I.

The Death of Cuchullin. 'United Ireland,' June 11. Reprinted in *The Countess Cathleen*, 1892. Also in *Poems*, 1895; and in the *Collected Works*, Vol. I.

[Michael Field's] *Sight and Song.* (A review.) 'The Bookman,' July.

The Irish Literary Society, London. (A letter.) 'United Ireland,' July 30.

Dublin Scholasticism and Trinity College. 'United Ireland,' July 30.

A New Poet. (Review of *Fate in Arcadia* by Edwin Ellis.) 'The Bookman,' September.

'Noetry' and Poetry. (Review of Savage Armstrong's collected verse.) 'The Bookman,' September.

The National Literary Society Libraries Scheme. (A letter.) 'United Ireland,' September 24.

A Mystical Prayer to the Masters of the Elements, Michael, Gabriel and Raphael. 'The Bookman,' Oct. Reprinted, under the title *A Mystical Prayer to the Masters of the Elements—Finvarra, Feacra, and Caolte*, in *The Second Book of the Rhymers' Club*, 1894.

Hopes and Fears for Irish Literature. 'United Ireland,' October 15.

The Rose in my Heart. 'The National Observer,' November 12. Reprinted in *The Second Book of the Rhymers' Club*, 1894. Also, under the title *Aedh tells of the Rose in his Heart*, in *The Wind Among the Reeds*, 1899; and in the *Collected Works*, Vol. I.

The Devil's Book. 'The National Observer,' November 26. Reprinted, under the title *The Book of the Great Dhoul and Hanrahan the Red*, in *The Secret Rose*, 1897.

[Tennyson's] *The Death of Œnone.* (A review.) 'The Bookman,' December.

The Fiddler of Dooney. 'The Bookman,' December. Reprinted in *The Second Book of the Rhymers' Club*, 1894. Also in *The Wind Among the Reeds*, 1899; and in the *Collected Works*, Vol. I.

The De-Anglicising of Ireland. (A letter.) 'United Ireland,' December 17.

The Twisting of the Rope. 'The National Observer,' December 24. Reprinted, under the title *The Twisting of the Rope and Hanrahan the Red*, in *The Secret Rose*, 1897.

1893.

[Kuno Meyer's] *The Vision of MacConglinne.* (A review.) *The Bookman.* February.

[Robert Buchanan's] *The Wandering Jew.* (A review.) 'The Bookman,' April.

The Heart of the Spring. 'The National Observer,' April 15. Reprinted in *The Secret Rose*, 1897; and in the *Collected Works*, Vol. VII.

The Danaan Quicken Tree. (A poem.) 'The Bookman,' May.

The Last Gleeman. 'The National Observer,' May 6. Reprinted in *The Celtic Twilight*, 1893 and 1902; and in the *Collected Works*, Vol. V.

Nationality and Literature. (A lecture to the National Literary Society.) 'United Ireland,' May 27.

Out of the Rose. 'The National Observer,' May 27. Reprinted in *The Secret Rose*, 1897; and in the *Collected Works*, Vol. VII.

The Celtic Twilight. 'The National Observer,' July 29. Reprinted, under the title *Into the Twilight*, in *The Celtic Twilight*, 1893 and 1902. Also in the *The Wind Among the Reeds*, 1899; and in the *Collected Works*, Vol. I.

The Writings of William Blake. (Review of a volume of *The Parchment Library*.) 'The Bookman,' August.

The Moods. 'The Bookman,' August. Reprinted in *The Celtic Twilight*, 1893 and 1902. Also in *The Wind Among the Reeds*, 1899; and in the *Collected Works*, Vol. I.

The Curse of the Fires and of the Shadows. 'The National Observer,' August 5. Reprinted in *The Secret Rose*, 1897; and in the *Collected Works*, Vol. VII.

The Message of the Folk-Lorist. 'The Speaker,' August 19.

Old Gaelic Love Songs. (Review of *The Love Songs of Connacht* by Douglas Hyde.) 'The Bookman,' Oct.

The Faery Host. 'The National Observer,' October 7. Reprinted, under the title *The Host*, in *The Celtic Twilight*, 1893. Also, under the title *The Hosting of the Sidhe*, in *The Wind Among the Reeds*, 1899; *The Celtic Twilight*, 1902; and in the *Collected Works*, Vol. I.

An Impression. 'The Speaker,' October 21. Reprinted, under the title *A Knight of the Sheep*, in *The Celtic Twilight*, 1893 and 1902; and in the *Collected Works*, Vol. V.

The Stolen Bride. 'The Bookman,' November. Reprinted, under the title *The Folk of the Air*, in *The Second Book of the Rhymers' Club*, 1894. Also, under the title *The Host of the Air*, in *The Wind Among the Reeds*, 1899; and in the *Collected Works*, Vol. I.

Our Lady of the Hills. 'The Speaker,' Nov. 11. Reprinted in *The Celtic Twilight*, 1893 and 1902; and in the *Collected Works*, Vol. V.

Wisdom and Dreams. (A poem.) 'The Bookman,' December.

Michael Clancy, the Great Dhoul, and Death. 'The Old Country,' a Christmas Annual, 1893.

The Celt: the Silenced Sister. (Two letters.) 'United Ireland,' December 23 and 30.

1894.

[E. J. Ellis's] *Seen in Three Days*. (A review.) 'The Bookman,' February.

Cap and Bell. 'The National Observer,' March 17. Reprinted, under the title *The Cap and Bells*, in *The Second Book of the Rhymers' Club*, 1894. Also in *The Wind Among the Reeds*, 1899; and in the *Collected Works*, Vol. I.

A Crucifixion. 'The National Observer,' March 24. Reprinted, under the title *The Crucifixion of the Outcast*, in *The Secret Rose*, 1897. Also in the *Collected Works*, Vol. VII.

The Song of the Old Mother. 'The Bookman,' April. Reprinted in *The Second Book of the Rhymers' Club*, 1894. Also in *The Wind Among the Reeds*, 1899; and in the *Collected Works*, Vol. I.

A Symbolical Drama in Paris. (Note on a performance of *Axel*.) 'The Bookman,' April.

The Evangel of Folklore. (Review of William Larminie's *West Irish Folk Tales*.) 'The Bookman,' June.

Those Who Live in the Storm. 'The Speaker,' July 21. Reprinted, under the title *The Rose of Shadow*, in *The Secret Rose*, 1897.

A New Poet. (Review of *Homeward* by A. E.) 'The Bookman,' August.

Kathleen-ny-Hoolihan. 'The National Observer,' Aug. 4. Reprinted, under the title *Kathleen the Daughter of Hoolihan and Hanrahan the Red*, in *The Secret Rose*, 1897.

The Curse of O'Sullivan the Red upon Old Age. 'The National Observer,' September 29. Reprinted, under the title *The Curse of Hanrahan the Red*, in *The Secret Rose*, 1897.

The Stone and the Elixir. (Review of Ibsen's *Brand*.) 'The Bookman,' October.

1895.

Battles Long Ago. (Review of Standish O'Grady's *The Coming of Cuchullain.*) 'The Bookman,' Feb.

An Excellent Talker. (Review of Oscar Wilde's *A Woman of No Importance.*) 'The Bookman,' March.

To Some I have talked with by the fire. 'The Bookman,' May. Reprinted in *Poems*, 1895. Also in the *Collected Works*, Vol. I.

Dublin Mystics. (Review of *Homeward* by A. E., and of *Two Essays on the Remnant* by John Eglinton.) 'The Bookman,' May.

[Douglas Hyde's] *The Story of Early Gaelic Literature.* (A review.) 'The Bookman,' June.

Irish National Literature. I. From Callanan to Carleton. 'The Bookman,' July.

[Douglas Hyde's] *The Three Sorrows of Story Telling.* (A review.) 'The Bookman,' July.

Irish National Literature. II. Contemporary Prose Writers. Mr. O'Grady, Miss Lawless, Miss Barlow, Miss Hopper and the Folk-Lorists. 'The Bookman,' Aug. The first paragraph of this essay is reprinted, under the title *The Moods*, in *Ideas of Good and Evil*, 1903. Also in the *Collected Works*, Vol. VI.

That Subtle Shade. (Review of *London Nights* by Arthur Symons.) 'The Bookman,' August.

Irish National Literature. III. Contemporary Irish Poets. Dr. Hyde, Mr. Rolleston, Mrs. Hinkson, Miss Nora Hopper, A. E., Mr. Aubrey de Vere, Dr. Todhunter and Mr. Lionel Johnson. 'The Bookman,' Sept. The first paragraph of this essay is reprinted, under the title *The Body of the Father Christian Rosencrux*, in *Ideas of Good and Evil*, 1903. Also in the *Collected Works*, Volume VI.

Wisdom. 'The New Review,' September. Reprinted, under the title *The Wisdom of the King*, in *The Secret Rose*, 1897. Also in the *Collected Works*, Vol. VII.

A Song of the Rosy Cross. 'The Bookman,' October.

Irish National Literature. IV. A List of the best Irish Books. 'The Bookman,' October.

[Dr. Todhunter's] *The Life of Patrick Sarsfield.* (A review.) 'The Bookman,' November.

The Twilight of Forgiveness. 'The Saturday Review,' November 2. Reprinted, under the title *Michael Robartes asks Forgiveness because of his many Moods*, in *The Wind Among the Reeds*, 1899. Also in the *Collected Works*, Vol. I.

St. Patrick and the Pedants. 'The Weekly Sun Literary Supplement,' December 1. Reprinted, under the title *The Old Men of the Twilight*, in *The Secret Rose*, 1897. Also in the *Collected Works*, Vol. VII.

1896.

The Shadowy Horses. 'The Savoy,' January. Reprinted, under the title *Michael Robartes bids his Beloved be at Peace*, in *The Wind Among the Reeds*, 1899. Also in the *Collected Works*, Vol. I. Translated into French by Stuart Merrill in *Vers et Prose*, March—May, 1905.

The Travail of Passion. 'The Savoy,' January. Reprinted in *The Wind Among the Reeds*, 1899. Also in the *Collected Works*, Vol. I. Translated into French by Stuart Merrill in *Vers et Prose*, March—May, 1905.

The Binding of the Hair. 'The Savoy,' January. Reprinted in *The Secret Rose*, 1897.

Everlasting Voices. 'The New Review,' January. Reprinted in *The Wind Among the Reeds*, 1899. Also in the *Collected Works*, Vol. I.

William Carleton. (Review of *The Life of William Carleton.*) 'The Bookman,' March.

O'Sullivan the Red to Mary Lavell. 'The Senate,' March. Two poems, reprinted, under the titles *Aedh tells of the perfect Beauty* and *A Poet to his Beloved*, in *The Wind Among the Reeds*, 1899. Also in the *Collected Works*, Vol. I.

Rosa Alchemica. 'The Savoy,' April. Reprinted in *The Secret Rose*, 1897. Also in the *Collected Works*, Vol. VII. Translated into French by Henry D. Davray in *Le Mercure de France*, October, 1898.

Two Poems concerning Peasant Visionaries:—I. *A Cradle Song.* II. *The Valley of the Black Pig.* 'The Savoy,' April. Reprinted in *The Wind Among the Reeds*, 1899. Also in the *Collected Works*, Vol. I.

Verlaine in 1894. 'The Savoy,' April.

The Vision of O'Sullivan the Red. 'The New Review,' April. Reprinted, under the title *The Vision of Hanrahan the Red*, in *The Secret Rose*, 1897.

William Blake. (Review of Dr. Richard Garnett's *William Blake* in 'The Portfolio' series of monographs.) 'The Bookman,' April.

An Irish Patriot. (Review of Lady Ferguson's *Sir Samuel Ferguson in the Ireland of his Day.*) 'The Bookman,' May.

The New Irish Library. (Review of *Swift in Ireland, Owen Roe O'Neill*, and *A Short Life of Thomas Davies.*) 'The Bookman,' June.

O'Sullivan Rua to Mary Lavell. 'The Savoy,' July. Reprinted, under the title *Michael Robartes remembers forgotten Beauty*, in *The Wind Among the Reeds*, 1899. Also in the *Collected Works*, Vol. I. Translated into French by Stuart Merrill in *Vers et Prose*, March—May, 1905.

William Blake and his Illustrations to the Divine Comedy. I. His Opinions upon Art. 'The Savoy,' July. Reprinted in *Ideas of Good and Evil*, 1903. Also in the *Collected Works*, Vol. VI.

La Tristesse du Berger. Trois légendes populaires d' Irlande. (Translations into French of *The Sad Shepherd* and *The Untiring Ones* by Henry D. Davray.) 'L'Ermitage,' July.

William Blake and his Illustrations to the Divine Comedy. II. His Opinions upon Dante. 'The Savoy,' Aug. Reprinted in *Ideas of Good and Evil*,

1903. Also in the *Collected Works*, Vol. VI.

William Blake and his Illustrations to the Divine Comedy. III. The Illustrations of Dante. 'The Savoy,' September. Reprinted in *Ideas of Good and Evil*, 1903. Also in the *Collected Works*, Vol. VI.

Greek Folk Poetry. (Review of Lucy M. Garnett's *Greek Folk Poesy.*) 'The Bookman,' October.

Where there is Nothing, there is God. 'The Sketch,' October 21. Reprinted in *The Secret Rose*, 1897. Also in the *Collected Works*, Vol. VII.

Windlestraws. 'The Savoy,' November. I. *O'Sullivan Rua to the Curlew.* Reprinted, under the title *Hanrahan reproves the Curlew*, in *The Wind Among the Reeds*, 1899. Also in the *Collected Works*, Vol. I. II. *Out of the Old Days.* Reprinted, under the title *To my Heart, bidding it have no Fear*, in *The Wind Among the Reeds*, 1899. Also in the *Collected Works*, Vol. I.

The Tables of the Law. 'The Savoy,' November. Reprinted in book form, 1897 and 1904. Also in the *Collected Works*, Vol. VII.

The Cradles of Gold. (A story.) 'The Senate,' Nov.

[William Morris's] *The Well at the World's End.* (A review.) 'The Bookman,' November.

Miss Fiona Macleod as a Poet. (Review of *From the Hills of Dream.*) 'The Bookman,' December.

The Death of O'Sullivan the Red. 'The New Review,' December. Reprinted, under the title *The Death of Hanrahan the Red*, in *The Secret Rose*, 1897.

Costello the Proud, Oona MacDermott and the Bitter Tongue. 'The Pageant,' 1896. Reprinted in *The Secret Rose*, 1897. Also in the *Collected Works*, Vol. VII.

1897.

[Sir Charles Gavan Duffy's] *Young Ireland.* (A review.) 'The Bookman,' January.

The Valley of Lovers. 'The Saturday Review,' Jan. 9. Reprinted, under the title *Aedh tells of a Valley full of Lovers*, in *The Wind Among the Reeds*, 1899. Also in the *Collected Works*, Vol. I.

John O'Leary. (Review of John O'Leary's *Recollections of Fenians and Fenianism*.) 'The Bookman,' Feb.

Mr. Arthur Symons's New Book. (Review of *Amoris Victima*.) 'The Bookman,' April.

The Blessed. 'The Yellow Book,' April. Reprinted in *The Wind Among the Reeds*, 1899. Also in the *Collected Works*, Vol. I.

Miss Fiona Macleod. (Review of *Spiritual Tales*, *Tragic Romances* and *Barbaric Tales*.) 'The Sketch,' April 28.

Robert Bridges. 'The Bookman,' June. Reprinted, under the title *The Return of Ulysses*, in *Ideas of Good and Evil*, 1903. Also in the *Collected Works*, Vol. VI.

The Desire of Man and of Woman. 'The Dome,' June. Reprinted, under the title *Mongan Laments the Change that has come upon him and his Beloved*, in *The Wind Among the Reeds*, 1899. Also in the *Collected Works*, Vol. I.

William Blake. 'The Academy,' June 19. Reprinted, under the title *William Blake and the Imagination*, in *Ideas of Good and Evil*, 1903. Also in the *Collected Works*, Vol. VI.

[Maurice Maeterlinck's] *The Treasure of the Humble.* (A review.) 'The Bookman,' July.

Song. 'The Saturday Review,' July 24. Reprinted, under the title *The Poet pleads with his Friend for old Friends*, in *The Wind Among the Reeds*, 1899. Also in the *Collected Works*, Vol. I.

Mr. Standish O'Grady's 'Flight of the Eagle.' (A review.) 'The Bookman,' August.

O'Sullivan the Red upon his Wanderings. 'The New Review,' August. Reprinted, under the title *Hanrahan Laments because of his Wanderings*, in *The Wind Among the Reeds*, 1899. Also, under the title *Maid Quiet*, in the *Collected Works*, Vol. I.

[Maurice Maeterlinck's] *Aglavaine and Selysette.* (A review.) 'The Bookman,' September.

The Tribes of Danu. 'The New Review,' November. Reprinted in part, under the title *The Friends of the People of Faery*, in *The Celtic Twilight*, 1902. Also in the *Collected Works*, Vol. V.

Three Irish Poets. (A.E., Nora Hopper and Lionel Johnson.) 'A Celtic Christmas,' December. (Christmas number of *The Irish Homestead*.)

1898.

The Prisoners of the Gods. 'The Nineteenth Century,' January.

Mr. Lionel Johnson's Poems. (Review of *Ireland; and other poems.*) 'The Bookman,' February.

Mr. Rhys' Welsh Ballads. (A review.) 'The Bookman,' April.

The Broken Gates of Death. 'The Fortnightly Review,' April.

Aodh to Dectora. Three Songs. 'The Dome,' May. Reprinted, under the titles *Aedh hears the Cry of the Sedge, Aedh Laments the Loss of Love,* and *Aedh thinks of those who have spoken Evil of his Beloved,* in *The Wind Among the Reeds,* 1899. Also in the *Collected Works,* Vol. I.

The Celtic Element in Literature. 'Cosmopolis,' June. Reprinted in *Ideas of Good and Evil,* 1903. Also in the *Collected Works,* Vol. VI.

Mr. Lionel Johnson and Certain Irish Poets. 'The Daily Express' (Dublin), August 27. Reprinted, under the title *Lionel Johnson,* in *A Treasury of Irish Poetry,* 1900. Also in the *Collected Works,* Vol. VIII.

Celtic Beliefs about the Soul. (Review of *The Voyage of Bran* by Kuno Meyer and Alfred Nutt.) 'The Bookman,' September.

The Poetry of A. E. 'The Daily Express' (Dublin), September 3. Reprinted, under the title '*A.E.,*' in *A Treasure of Irish Poetry,* 1900.

The Poems and Stories of Miss Nora Hopper. 'The Daily Express' (Dublin), September 24. Reprinted in part, under the title *A Note on National Drama,* in *Literary Ideals in Ireland,* 1899; and in part, under the title *Nora Hopper,* in *A Treasury of Irish Poetry,* 1900.

Song of Mongan. 'The Dome,' October. Reprinted, under the title *Mongan thinks of his past Greatness,* in *The Wind Among the Reeds,* 1899. Also in the *Collected Works,* Vol. I.

Rosa Alchemica. (French Translation.) 'Le Mercure de France,' October.

John Eglinton and Spiritual Art. 'The Daily Express' (Dublin), October, 29. Reprinted in *Literary Ideals in Ireland,* 1899.

A Symbolic Artist and the Coming of Symbolic Art. 'The Dome,' December.

Aodh Pleads with the Elemental Powers. 'The Dome,' December. Reprinted in *The Wind Among the Reeds,* 1899. Also in the *Collected Works,* Vol. I.

Bressel the Fisherman. 'The Cornish Magazine,' Dec. Reprinted in *The Wind Among the Reeds,* 1899. Also in the *Collected Works,* Vol. I.

The Autumn of the Flesh. 'The Daily Express' (Dublin), December 3. Reprinted in *Literary Ideals in Ireland,* 1899. Also under the title *The Autumn of the Body* in *Ideas of Good and Evil,* 1903; and in the *Collected Works,* Vol. VI.

1899.

The Irish Literary Theatre. 'The Daily Express' (Dublin), Jan. 14. Reprinted in part, under the title *Plans and Methods*, in 'Beltaine', May, 1899.

Mr. Moore, Mr. Archer and the Literary Theatre. (A letter, dated January 27, 1899.) 'The Daily Chronicle,' January 30.

The Academic Class and the Agrarian Revolution. 'The Daily Express' (Dublin), March 11.

The Theatre. 'The Dome,' April. Reprinted in 'Beltaine,' May, 1899. Also in *Ideas of Good and Evil*, 1903; and in the *Collected Works*, Vol. VI.

Plans and Methods. 'Beltaine,' May.

The Irish Literary Theatre. 'Literature,' May 6.

The Countess Cathleen and Cardinal Logue. (A letter.) 'The Morning Leader,' May 13.

[Fiona Macleod's] *The Dominion of Dreams.* (A review.) 'The Bookman,' July.

Ireland Bewitched. 'The Contemporary Review,' September.

'Dust hath closed Helen's Eye.' 'The Dome,' October. Reprinted in *The Celtic Twilight*, 1902. Also in the *Collected Works*, Vol. V.

The Literary Movement in Ireland. 'The North American Review,' December. Reprinted in *Ideals in Ireland*, 1901.

1900.

The Irish Literary Theatre, 1900. 'The Dome,' Jan. Reprinted in 'Beltaine,' February, 1900. A paragraph is also reprinted, as part of the essay *The Theatre*, in *Ideas of Good and Evil*, 1903; and in the *Collected Works*, Vol. VI.

Plans and Methods. 'Beltaine,' February.

'Maive' and Certain Irish Beliefs. 'Beltaine,' Feb.

The Symbolism of Poetry. 'The Dome,' April. Reprinted in *Ideas of Good and Evil*, 1903. Also in the *Collected Works*, Vol. VI.

'The Last Feast of the Fianna,' 'Maive,' and 'The Bending of the Bough' in Dublin. 'Beltaine,' April.

The Way of Wisdom. 'The Speaker,' April 14. Reprinted, under the title *The Pathway*, in the *Collected Works*, Vol. VIII.

The Shadowy Waters. 'The North American Review,' May. Reprinted in book form, 1900. A new version of the play is printed in *Poems*, 1899-1905; and in the *Collected Works*, Vol. II.; and an acting version in book form, 1907, and in the *Collected Works*, Vol. II.

The Philosophy of Shelley's Poetry. 'The Dome,' July. Reprinted in *Ideas of Good and Evil*, 1903. Also in the *Collected Works*, Vol. VI.

The Freedom of the Press in Ireland. (A letter.) 'The Speaker,' July 7.

Irish Fairy Beliefs. (A review of Daniel Deeny's *Peasant Lore from Gaelic Ireland*.) 'The Speaker,' July 14.

Irish Language and Irish Literature. (A letter.) 'The Leader,' September 1.

Irish Witch Doctors. 'The Fortnightly Review,' Sept.

Introduction to a Dramatic Poem. 'The Speaker.' December 1. Reprinted without title in *The Shadowy Waters*, 1900. Also in *Poems*, 1899-1905; and in the *Collected Works*, Vol. II.

1901.

Cantilation. (A letter.) 'The Saturday Review,' March 16.

At Stratford-on-Avon. 'The Speaker,' May 11 and 18. Reprinted, with one chapter omitted, in *Ideas of Good and Evil*, 1903. Also in the *Collected Works*, Vol. VI.

The Fool of Faery. 'The Kensington,' June. Reprinted, under the title *The Queen and the Fool*, in *The Celtic Twilight*, 1902. Also in the *Collected Works*, Vol. V.

Under the Moon. 'The Speaker,' June 15. Reprinted in *In the Seven Woods*, 1903. Also in *Poems*, 1899-1905; and in the *Collected Works*, Vol. I.

Ireland and the Arts. 'The United Irishman,' Aug. 31. Reprinted in *Ideas of Good and Evil*, 1903. Also in the *Collected Works*, Vol. VI.

Magic. 'The Monthly Review,' September. Reprinted in *Ideas of Good and Evil*, 1903. Also in the *Collected Works*, Vol. VI.

Windlestraws. 'Samhain,' October. Reprinted in *The Irish Dramatic Movement*, *Collected Works*, Vol. IV.

1902.

The Blood Bond. (From *Grania* by George Moore and W. B. Yeats.) 'A Broad Sheet,' January.

Spinning Song. 'A Broad Sheet,' January.

The Folly of Being Comforted. 'The Speaker,' Jan. 11. Reprinted in *In the Seven Woods*, 1903. Also in *Poems*, 1899-1905; and in the *Collected Works*, Vol. I.

New Chapters in the Celtic Twilight. I. *Enchanted Woods.* 'The Speaker,' January 18. Reprinted in *The Celtic Twilight*, 1902. Also in the *Collected Works*, Vol. V.

Egyptian Plays. (A note on the performance of *The Beloved of Hathor* and *The Shrine of the Golden Hawk* by Florence Farr and O. Shakespear.) 'The Star,' January 23.

New Chapters in the Celtic Twilight. II. *Happy and Unhappy Theologians.* 'The Speaker,' Feb. 15. Reprinted in *The Celtic Twilight*, 1902. Also in the *Collected Works*, Vol. V.

What is 'Popular Poetry'? 'The Cornhill Magazine,' March. Reprinted in *Ideas of Good and Evil*, 1903. Also in the *Collected Works*, Vol. VI.

The Purcell Society. (A letter.) 'The Saturday Review,' March 8.

New Chapters in the Celtic Twilight. III. *The Old Town.* IV. *War.* V. *Earth, Fire and Water.* 'The Speaker,' March 15. Reprinted in *The Celtic Twilight*, 1902. Also in the *Collected Works*, Vol. V.

Away. 'The Fortnightly Review,' April.

The Acting at St. Teresa's Hall. (Notes on the performance of *Deirdre* by A.E., and of *Cathleen ni Hoolihan*.) 'The United Irishman,' April 12 and 19.

New Chapters in the Celtic Twilight. V. *A Voice.* VI. *The Swine of the Gods.* VII. *The Devil.* VIII. *'And Fair Fierce Women.'* IX. *Mortal Help.* 'The Speaker,' April 19. Reprinted in *The Celtic Twilight*, 1902. Also in the *Collected Works*, Vol. V.

New Chapters in the Celtic Twilight. X. *Aristotle of the Books.* XI. *Miraculous Creatures.* XII. *An Enduring Heart.* 'The Speaker,' April 26. Reprinted in *The Celtic Twilight*, 1902. Also in the *Collected Works*, Vol. V.

Speaking to the Psaltery. 'The Monthly Review,' May. Reprinted in *Ideas of Good and Evil*, 1903. Also in the *Collected Works*, Vol. VI.

Speaking to Musical Notes. (A letter.) 'The Academy,' June 7.

Baile and Aillinn. 'The Monthly Review,' July. Reprinted in *In the Seven Woods*, 1903. Also in *Poems*, 1899-1905; and in the *Collected Works*, Vol. I.

Notes. 'Samhain,' October. Reprinted in *The Irish Dramatic Movement*, *Collected Works*, Vol. IV.

Cathleen-ni-Hoolihan. 'Samhain,' October. Reprinted in book form, 1902. Also in *Plays for an Irish Theatre*, Vol. II., 1904; and in the *Collected Works*, Vol. IV.

The Freedom of the Theatre. 'The United Irishman,' November 1.

Adam's Curse. 'The Monthly Review,' December. Reprinted in *In the Seven Woods*, 1903. Also in *Poems*, 1899-1905; and in the *Collected Works*, Vol. I.

1903.

The Old Men admiring themselves in the Water. 'The Pall Mall Magazine,' January. Reprinted in *In the Seven Woods*, 1903. Also in *Poems*, 1899-1905; and in the *Collected Works*, Vol. I.

The Happiest of the Poets. 'The Fortnightly Review,' March. Reprinted in *Ideas of Good and Evil*, 1903. Also in the *Collected Works*, Vol. VI.

Poets and Dreamers. 'The New Liberal Review,' March. Reprinted, under the title *The Galway Plains*, in *Ideas of Good and Evil*, 1903. Also in the *Collected Works*, Vol. VI.

The Old Age of Queen Maeve. 'The Fortnightly Review,' April. Reprinted in *In the Seven Woods*, 1903. Also in *Poems*, 1899-1905; and in the *Collected Works*, Vol. I.

Cathleen, the Daughter of Hoolihan. 'A Broad Sheet,' April. Reprinted, under the title *The Song of Red Hanrahan*, in *In the Seven Woods*, 1903. Also in *Poems*, 1899-1905; and in the *Collected Works*, Vol. I.

The Reform of the Theatre. 'The United Irishman,' April 4. Reprinted, with additions, in 'Samhain,' September, 1903. Also in *The Irish Dramatic Movement, Collected Works*, Vol. IV.

Irish Plays and Players. (A letter.) 'The Academy,' May 16.

The Happy Townland. 'The Weekly Critical Review,' June. Reprinted, under the title *The Rider from the North*, in *In the Seven Woods*, 1903. Also, under original title, in *Poems*, 1899-1905; and in the *Collected Works*, Vol. I.

The Hour-Glass. A Morality. 'The North American Review,' September. Reprinted separately, for copyright purposes, in 1903. Also in *Plays for an Irish Theatre*, Vol. III., 1904; and in the *Collected Works*, Vol. IV.

Notes. 'Samhain,' September. Reprinted in *The Irish Dramatic Movement, Collected Works*, Vol. IV.

A Prologue. 'The United Irishman,' September 9. Reprinted in *Plays for an Irish Theatre*, Vol. III., 1904. Also in the *Collected Works*, Vol. VIII.

Flaubert and the National Library. (A letter.) *The Irish Times*, October 8.

An Irish National Theatre. 'The United Irishman,' October 10. Reprinted in *The Irish Dramatic Movement, Collected Works*, Vol. IV.

The Theatre, the Pulpit and the Newspapers. 'The United Irishman,' October 17. Reprinted in *The Irish Dramatic Movement, Collected Works*, Vol. IV.

The Irish National Theatre and Three Sorts of Ignorance. 'The United Irishman,' October 24.

Dream of the World's End. 'The Green Sheaf,' No. II.[K]

Red Hanrahan. 'The Independent Review,' Dec. Reprinted in *Stories of Red Hanrahan*, 1904. Also in the *Collected Works*, Vol. V.

1904.

The Dramatic Movement.

First Principles.

The Play, the Player and the Scene. 'Samhain,' Dec. Reprinted in *The Irish Dramatic Movement, Collected Works*, Vol. IV.

1905.

[J. M. Synge's] *The Shadow of the Glen.* (Three letters.) 'The United Irishman,' January 28, February 4 and 11.

Red Hanrahan's Vision. 'McClure Magazine,' March. Reprinted in *Stories of Red Hanrahan*, 1904. Also in the *Collected Works*, Vol. V.

America and the Arts. 'The Metropolitan Magazine,' April.

Trois Poèmes d' Amour. Les Chevaux de l'ombre. Le Travail de la Passion. O'Sullivan Rua à Marie Lavell. (French translations by Stuart Merrill.) *Vers et Prose*, March—May.

Queen Edaine. 'McClure's Magazine,' September. Reprinted with an additional verse in 'The Shanachie' [No. I., Spring, 1906.] Also in *Poems*, 1899-1905; *Deirdre*, 1907; and in the *Collected Works*, Vol. II.

Do not love too long. 'The Acorn,' October. Reprinted in the *Collected Works*, Vol. I.

Notes and Opinions. 'Samhain,' November. Reprinted in *The Irish Dramatic Movement, Collected Works*, Vol. IV.

Never Give All the Heart. 'McClure's Magazine,' December. Reprinted in *Poems*, 1899-1905; and in the *Collected Works*, Vol. I.

1906.

Against Witchcraft. 'The Shanachie,' Spring. Reprinted in *On Baile's Strand*, in *Poems*, 1899-1905. Also in the *Collected Works*, Vol. II.

The Praise of Deirdre. 'The Shanachie,' Spring. See *Queen Edaine*, above. (1905.)

My Thoughts and My Second Thoughts. I.-X. 'The Gentleman's Magazine,' September and October. Reprinted in *Discoveries*, 1907. Also in the *Collected Works*, Vol. VIII.

Literature and the Living Voice. 'The Contemporary Review,' October. Reprinted in 'Samhain,' 1906. Also in *The Irish Dramatic Movement, Collected Works*, Vol. IV.

The Season's Work. 'The Arrow,' October 20. Reprinted, in part, in *The Irish Dramatic Movement, Collected Works*, Vol. IV.

A Note on 'The Mineral Workers,' and other Notes. 'The Arrow,' October 20.

My Thoughts and My Second Thoughts. XI.-XVII. 'The Gentleman's Magazine,' November. Reprinted in *Discoveries*, 1907. Also in the *Collected Works*, Vol. VIII.

Notes.

Notes on 'Deirdre' and *'The Shadowy Waters.'* 'The Arrow,' November 24.

Notes. 'Samhain,' December.

1907.

The Controversy over 'The Playboy.'

Mr. Yeats' Opening Speech at the Debate on February 4th, at the Abbey Theatre. 'The Arrow,' February 23. Both reprinted, in part, in *The Irish Dramatic Movement, Collected Works*, Vol. IV.

Notes. 'The Arrow,' June 1. Reprinted in part, under the title *On Bringing 'The Playboy' to London*, in *The Irish Dramatic Movement, Collected Works*, Vol. IV.

Discoveries. 'The Shanachie,' October. Reprinted in *Discoveries*, 1907. Also in the *Collected Works*, Vol. VIII.

1908.

A Dream. (A poem, with a note in prose.) 'The Nation,' July 11.

PART IV.

AMERICAN EDITIONS.
(COMPILED BY JOHN QUINN.)

[1892.]

The | Countess Kathleen | And Various Legends and Lyrics. | By | W. B. Yeats. | [Quotation, four lines] | Cameo Series | Boston: Roberts Bros. | London: T. Fisher Unwin.

Identical with English edition except for title-page and publisher's name on back of binding and absence of publisher's device on back cover.

1894.

The | Land of Heart's Desire | By | W. B. Yeats | [publisher's monogram] | Chicago | Stone & Kimball | Caxton Building | MDCCCXCIV

Fcp. 8vo, pp. iv and 46. Grey boards with label. The frontispiece is by Aubrey Beardsley, the design being the same as that used in the English edition.

1903. Mosher's first edition.

The Land of Heart's Desire | By | W. B. Yeats | O Rose, thou art sick. | William Blake.

Sm. 4to. This is No. 6 of Vol. IX. of *The Bibelot*, issued in June, 1903. Grey paper cover.

The Land of Heart's Desire | By W. B. Yeats | [ornament] | Portland Maine | Privately Printed | MDCCCCIII

Fcp. 8vo, pp. xvi and 32. Japan paper cover.

Only 32 copies were printed, during July, 1903.

The Land of Heart's | Desire by William | Butler Yeats | [monogram] | Portland Maine | Thomas B. Mosher | MDCCCCIII

Sm. 8vo, pp. vi and 36. White parchment paper.

Of this first edition 950 copies were printed on Van Gelder paper, 100 on Japan paper and 10 on pure vellum. Published in October, 1903. Later editions, each consisting of 950 copies on Van Gelder paper, are bound in grey boards with paper label.

The Celtic Twilight. | Men and Women, Dhouls and | Faeries. | By W. B. Yeats. | With a frontispiece by J. B. Yeats. | New York: | Macmillan and Co. | and London. | 1894

English sheets, with new title-page.

1895.

Poems.

Copies of the English edition were imported by Copeland and Day of Boston, whose name appears on the title-page and binding of all copies.

1897.

The Secret Rose: | By W. B. Yeats, with | Illustrations by J. B. | Yeats. | [monogram] | New York: Dodd, Mead & Company | London: Lawrence and Bullen, Ltd. | MDCCCXCVII.

These copies for the American market are copies of the first English edition, with the original title-page torn out after the book was bound, and the above new title-page pasted in.

1899.

The Wind | Among the Reeds | By | W. B. Yeats | [ornament] | John Lane:
The Bodley Head | New York and London | 1899

Cr. 8vo, pp. viii and 110. Cloth.

The English edition was printed from duplicate plates and is identical except for imprint on title-page
and the cutting out of copyright notice and imprint on verso of title-page (p. [iv]) and the imprint at end
(p. [109]).

Later American editions have separate copyright notice on verso of title-page dated 1905 but are
printed from the same plates and contain no additional lines.

1901.

The Shadowy Waters | By | W. B. Yeats | [ornament] | New York | Dodd, Mead and Company | 1901

Cr. 4to, pp. 62. Grey boards with side label.

1902.

Where There is | Nothing | A Drama | In Five Acts | By | W. B. Yeats; John Lane | MCMII

Cr. 8vo, pp. viii and 100. Issued in grey paper cover, the first page printed from the types of the title-page.

Fifteen copies printed for copyright of which not over eight are now known. Printed for Mr. John Quinn from the author's first draft and contains some errors corrected in the large-paper edition.

1902. Second Edition.

Printed for Mr. John Quinn from the same types as the preceding, but without the publisher's name on title-page and without imprint on verso of title-page below copyright, and with some errors corrected. On the reverse of the half-title is the notice "Thirty copies printed | from the type, of which | this is No._____"

Large-paper copies ($9^9/_{16}$ths by $5^7/_{16}$ths inches). Pale green boards with labels on front and back.

These two editions contain a dedication to Lady Gregory, dated September 19, 1902, which does not appear in any subsequent edition.

1903. Third Edition.

Where There is | Nothing | Being Volume One of Plays for | an Irish Theatre | By | W. B. Yeats | New York | The Macmillan Company | London: Macmillan & Co., Ltd. | 1903 | All rights reserved

Globe 8vo, pp. 216. Cloth.

This edition was considerably revised and contains some new passages. The new dedication to Lady Gregory is dated February, 1903.

Also a large-paper edition, printed on Japan paper, and limited to 100 copies.

The Celtic Twilight. Revised and enlarged edition of 1902.

The English sheets were imported and bound in America, back of cover being lettered "The Celtic | Twilight | W. B. Yeats. | The Macmillan | Company"

1903.

Ideas of Good and | Evil. By W. B. Yeats | The Macmillan Company | New York. MCMIII

English sheets with new title-page as above.

In the Seven Woods | Being Poems Chiefly of the | Irish Heroic Age | By | W. B. Yeats | New York | The Macmillan Company | London: Macmillan & Co., Ltd. | 1903 | All rights reserved

Cr. 8vo, pp. vi and 90. Cloth.

1904.

The Hour-Glass | And Other Plays | Being Volume Two of Plays for | An Irish Theatre | By | W. B. Yeats | New York | The Macmillan Company | London: Macmillan & Co., Ltd. | 1904 | All rights reserved

Globe 8vo, pp. viii and 116. Cloth.[L]

Also a large-paper edition, limited to 100 copies.

These American editions do not contain the bars of music or the "Note on the Music" of the English edition.

The King's Threshold | A Play in Verse | By | W. B. Yeats | New York | Printed for Private Circulation | 1904

Medium 8vo, pp. x and 58. Grey boards.

Printed on cream-coloured old hand-made Italian paper, 100 copies only, for Mr. John Quinn.

1906.

The Poetical Works | of | William B. Yeats | In Two Volumes | Volume I | Lyrical Poems | New York | The Macmillan Company | London: Macmillan & Co., Ltd. | 1906 | All rights reserved

Cr. 8vo, pp. xiv and 340. Cloth.

CONTENTS.

Preface. [Dated *In the Seven Woods*, July, 1906.]

Early Poems: I. Ballads and Lyrics.

Early Poems: II. The Wanderings of Oisin.

Early Poems: III. The Rose.

The Wind Among the Reeds.

In the Seven Woods.

The Old Age of Queen Maeve.

Baile and Aillinn.

1907.

The Poetical Works | of | William B. Yeats | In Two Volumes | Volume II | Dramatical Poems | New York | The Macmillan Company | London: Macmillan & Co., Ltd. | 1907 | All rights reserved

Cr. 8vo, pp. x and 528.

CONTENTS.

Preface. [Dated December, 1906.]

The Countess Cathleen.

The Land of Heart's Desire.

The Shadowy Waters. [New version.]

On Baile's Strand. [New version.]

The King's Threshold. [New version.]

Deirdre.

Appendix I: The Legendary and Mythological Foundation of the Plays and Poems.

Appendix II: The Dates and Places of Performance of the Plays.

Appendix III: Acting Version of 'The Shadowy Waters.'

Appendix IV: The Work of the National Theatre Society at the Abbey Theatre, Dublin: A Statement of Principles.

These two volumes form the first collected edition of the author's verse, lyric and dramatic. It is to America's credit that this first collected edition appeared in America.

1908.

The Unicorn from | the Stars | and Other Plays | By | William B. Yeats | and | Lady Gregory | New York | The Macmillan Company | 1908 | All rights reserved

Cr. 8vo, pp. xiv and 210. Cloth.

CONTENTS.

The Unicorn from the Stars. By Lady Gregory and W. B. Yeats.

Cathleen ni Hoolihan.

The Hour-Glass: A Morality.

The Golden Helmet | By | William Butler Yeats | Published | By | John Quinn | New York 1908

Fcp. 8vo, pp. viii and 34. Grey boards with label.

Fifty copies only printed.

NOTE.

Of the first separate edition of *The Hour-Glass*, described in Part I. under date 1903, only twelve copies were printed. Of these, six went for English copyright, two were lost in the post, the printer kept one, one belongs to Mr. W. B. Yeats, one to Lady Gregory and one to Mr. John Quinn.

The essay *Modern Irish Poetry*, which appeared as an Introduction to *A Book of Irish Verse*, London, 1895 (see Part II.), was reissued with additions in *Irish Literature*, Vol. III., Philadelphia, 1904.

THE END.

———————————————

Printed by A. H. B<small>ULLEN</small>, *at The Shakespeare Head Press,*
Stratford-on-Avon.

FOOTNOTES:

[A] *Poems of Spenser: Selected and with an Introduction by W. B. Yeats.* (T. C. and E. C. Jack, Edinburgh, N.D.)

[B] Rose Kavanagh, the poet, wrote to her religious adviser from, I think, Leitrim, where she lived, and asked him to get her the works of Mazzini. He replied, 'You must mean Manzone.'

[C] I have heard him say more than once, 'I will not say our people know good from bad, but I will say that they don't hate the good when it is pointed out to them as a great many people do in England.'

[D] A small political organizer told me once that he and a certain friend got together somewhere in Tipperary a great meeting of farmers for O'Leary on his coming out of prison, and O'Leary had said at it: 'The landlords gave us some few leaders, and I like them for that, and the artisans have given us great numbers of good patriots, and so I like them best: but you I do not like at all, for you have never given us any one.' I have known but one that had his moral courage, and that was a woman with beauty, to give her courage and self-possession.

[E] This version, though Dr. Hyde went some way with it, has never been published. I do not know why.—W.B.Y., *March, 1908.*

[F] Reprinted from *The Wanderings of Oisin*, 1889.

[G] Reprinted from *The Countess Cathleen*, 1892.

[H] Written for the first production of *The King's Threshold* in Dublin, but not used, as, owing to the smallness of the company, nobody could be spared to speak it.—W.B.Y., 1904.

[I] Reprinted from *The Shadowy Waters*, 1900.

[J] Reprinted from *In the Seven Woods*, 1903.

[K] 'The Green Sheaf,' No. IV., published as a supplement a reproduction of a pastel by Mr. Yeats, *The Lake at Coole.*

[L] *The Pot of Broth*, contained in this volume, originally appeared in *The Gael*, (an American Monthly Magazine, printed in New York, partly in Irish and partly in English,) September, 1903.

www.ingramcontent.com/pod-product-compliance
Lightning Source LLC
Chambersburg PA
CBHW020813060726
47498CB00017B/2772